★

The street was already blocked off by several police cars, their lights flashing, drenching the area in a red glow. A few neighbors had come out of their houses to see what was happening. The cab let us off across the street and we walked over to the nearest policeman.

"Is she all right?" I asked.

"Is who all right, ma'am?" he asked. "Do you know something about this situation?"

"I was the one who called it in. Is she all right? Did you get here in time?"

The officer let Raina and me through, then ordered me to stand on the perimeter of the crime scene while he got the detective to come talk to me.

I didn't need the young patrolman or Detective Sturgeon to tell me one thing: the body bag made it official.

★

Previously published Worldwide Mystery title by
WENDI LEE

MISSING EDEN

Deadbeat

WENDI LEE

WORLDWIDE.

TORONTO • NEW YORK • LONDON
AMSTERDAM • PARIS • SYDNEY • HAMBURG
STOCKHOLM • ATHENS • TOKYO • MILAN
MADRID • WARSAW • BUDAPEST • AUCKLAND

DEADBEAT

A Worldwide Mystery/February 2000

First published by St. Martin's Press, Incorporated.

ISBN 0-373-26339-2

Visit us at www.worldwidemystery.com

Printed in U.S.A.

Acknowledgments

I would like to thank the following people: Barbara Peuchner, Mary Kay Lane, Matt Clemens, Michael Black, Mari Famulari, Peter "Chink" Cardinale, Brent Bowen, Dan Rohde, Keith Kahla, and S. J. Rozan. Also very supportive during the gestation period of this book were Judy Taylor, Mary Campbell, Chris Weir, R. Judith Vincent, and Nancy Harrison.

ONE

CYNTHIA MACDONALD didn't wear her Anne Klein power suit so much as she wielded it. Her body language made it clear that she would feel more comfortable sitting behind my desk than in the client's chair—she was obviously better at being the interviewer than being interviewed—and I hazarded a guess that she worked for some large, faceless corporation. Cynthia MacDonald had been here for ten minutes and I couldn't even venture a guess at why she was here. For a woman with a problem that only a private investigator could handle, she hadn't told me a damn thing. So far, she'd spent most of that time asking about my background, and the only thing we hadn't covered was my personal life.

"So tell me, Ms. Matelli," Ms. MacDonald said now, sitting back in the straight-back chair, "why did you become a private investigator?"

"It was what I was qualified to do after I left the Marines," I replied.

When I joined the Marines, I was lousy at typing, so they couldn't stick me in the typing pool with the other BAMs, short for Big Ass Marine—not something a male marine wants to call a female marine to her face—so I was assigned to assisting a major. Basically, I drove him around, ran errands, and ran interference for him in certain touchy situations. But the major and I were attracted to one another, and although we kept it on a friendly basis, his wife didn't like me. When she made a big stink about "that BAM slut who's assisting my husband," I was reassigned. Fortunately, the major gave me free rein to choose my next assignment. I chose the Military Police. It wasn't long before I was a sergeant in charge of investigations. But I wasn't about to go into all that detail. Telling Cynthia MacDonald that I'd been in the Marines was enough.

In fact, she beamed at me and nodded approvingly. "A marine? You must be made of tough stuff, then."

I smiled confidently, then took a sip of my cappuccino and burned my tongue. Being the tough marine that I was, I didn't wince in my client's presence. I'd recently had a birthday, and Ma had given me a cappuccino machine. Of course she had bought it at a discount from one of her myriad relatives.

I have three brothers, Ray, Vinnie, and Albert, and two sisters, Sophia and Rosa. My sisters have apartments in the building I own—Rosa lives on the second floor and Sophia and her two kids will soon be moving out of their temporary digs on the first floor. I'm the middle sister, and in the whole family, I rank fourth. Rosa and Albert are younger than me and, except for Ray, Rosa's the only one who's attending college—the University of Massachusetts. Ma took Rosa's choice of major, art history, pretty well. She shrugged and told her, "Well, at least you'll have a chance to meet Mr. Right while you're still in college. Unlike your sister." Ma was referring to me. Her fondest wish, when I was in the Marines, was that I would meet my Mr. Right and marry him, have babies, and not reenlist. But we all love Ma, despite her Old World views.

Which brings me back to the cappuccino maker. Ma had figured that it would add a little polish to my tiny office and would attract a better class of clientele. Of course, she dreams that someday soon a wealthy client will come in and, during the meeting with me, notice that I made wonderful cappuccino. He'll ask me out, we'll fall in love, marry, I'll give up the private-eye business, and have babies. Cynthia MacDonald was suitably impressed. But I hoped she wouldn't ask me out on a date. She wasn't my type.

The cappuccino maker also had the added benefit of attracting my neighbors in the office building. It was nice to get to know them, although in some cases, I wasn't sure if it was a benefit at all. The smell of fresh-brewed Italian roast permeated the hallways outside my office and wafted past the delicate olfactory senses of the Romanian cross-dressing dentist, Dan Something-or-Other (his name was unpronounceable in my book, but it had a lot of Xs and Ys in it), and a bail bondsman by the name of Bennie the Bond, who seemed to know everyone I knew. I'd never heard of the guy till I got my cappuccino maker.

While my mind wandered, Cynthia MacDonald continued to prattle on. I tuned in again, wondering if she had noticed the glazed look in my eyes.

"I suppose that's why I became a stockbroker." She smiled for the first time, as if allowing herself that luxury. "I'm good at numbers and projecting the future of a stock. It seemed to have been the path for me to take at the time." Her smile turned ironic. Ironic: that was a five-dollar word I'd learned from my little sister Rosa, the college girl.

"Are you married, Ms. Matelli?" Cynthia Mac-Donald crossed her thick ankles and cocked her head, leaning forward. If I had been a man and she had been a reasonably attractive woman, I might have been interested in the gap in her ivory silk blouse beneath the red suit jacket. But it was clear to me that Cynthia MacDonald had risen to whatever power position she held by her brains and her ambition. The prominent mole on the left side of her bulbous nose could not be called a beauty mark by any standard, and her colorless eyes had short, colorless lashes. She hadn't even attempted to put makeup on, probably because she knew it wouldn't help. Her only stunning feature was the lustrous dark-auburn hair that was swept up in a shining mass of curls.

"What does my marital status have to do with anything?" In my opinion, the only person who has any right to ask whether I am single or married is

Ma. And as I explained, she wields her power over me like a guillotine.

My potential client looked a bit taken aback by my sharp tone, but then she waved a hand. "I just want to be thorough. If you're married, you might have commitments that would stand in the way of taking on this case."

I sent a frozen smile back to her. "Most private investigators do their job regardless of their marital status. I just don't want you to get the impression that simply because I'm a woman in this business, I can't do the job because of a husband and kid at home." She had taken up enough of my time with her anal-retentive thoroughness.

Although I could use a case that didn't involve picking up a repo from in front of a steroid user's house in Chelsea, I didn't need a case this badly. The truth of the matter was that I was bored, bored with the bread-and-butter stuff I'd been doing lately—repos, and investigating the insurance claims, and serving summonses on occasion. I wanted a real case. I just hoped there was promise here, not merely some woman who wanted to see if her fiancé was being faithful.

"What exactly are you looking for?" I finally asked.

She closed her eyes, propped her elbows on the arms of the chair, and made a steeple with her fingers. "I need you to find me."

If my ears could have done a double take, they would have. "Excuse me. You did say you wanted me to find you?'' The lyrics to that awful '80s song, ''I've Never Been to Me,'' forced their way into my head. It was unrelenting, and when this woman left my office, I would have to fill my ears with some good music—maybe Elvis Costello or Bonnie Raitt.

A faint, wry twist of her mouth and a nod left no doubt that this was what she wanted. ''It sounds bizarre, I know. Let me explain.''

''By all means.'' I leaned back gingerly in my office chair. The chair was like a cantankerous bucking horse—several times I'd leaned too far back and had been unceremoniously dumped out of it. But the saying, ''If you get bucked from a horse once, you need to get right back on it,'' applied to that chair, and so I was back in the saddle again.

''Recently, I was at Tech City in Quincy to buy a big-screen television, and I applied for instant credit.'' She paused for effect. ''I was turned down.''

I raised my eyebrows. ''Everyone gets turned down for credit once in a while.''

She shook her head. ''You don't understand. The guy at Tech City told me that I already had credit with them, and that I had passed my credit limit.''

''Could you have gotten credit from Tech City a while ago and forgotten?''

Cynthia MacDonald began to drum her fingernails on the arm of the chair. ''No. That's not possible. I keep very good records of my transactions and my creditors.''

''And it wasn't just a mistake on their part?'' I

ventured. "Possibly a different Cynthia MacDonald?"

"The address was different, and the phone number. I had them verify that much for me. But the Social Security number was the clincher." She'd been looking off to my left. Now she looked straight at me. "It was my number." She paused, as if waiting for the *da-da-da daaa* to accompany her revelation, but when it didn't, she continued: "I decided to have my secretary do a little digging into my credit background, and that's when I discovered that my credit record was a mess."

Trust a woman boss to have her secretary do all the work while she takes all the credit for the discovery. "Get in line. Half the population has a messy credit record," I said, putting my empty cappuccino cup down.

Cynthia MacDonald sighed impatiently. "You don't understand. There are credit cards on my file that don't have an iota of credit left on them." She opened her briefcase and pulled out a thick file folder, setting it down between us. "And they're all cards I never applied for.

"My name is on accounts with stores all over the New England area. We discover a new account almost every day. I owe thousands to credit companies." She leaned forward for the full impact of her words to hit me. "I didn't open those accounts and I'm not paying for them. At this point, I'll be ruined inside of a month. The other Cynthia MacDonald has rung up a total of seventy-five thousand dollars already, and not all the bills are in yet. Will you take my case?"

I frowned. It sounded as if someone was using her name and Social Security number. Interesting. "Okay, Ms. MacDonald—"

"Please call me Cynthia," she said. I could see the release of tension in her shoulders.

I hadn't really decided to take her case, but it would have been awkward to explain that I was just going to say, "Okay, Cynthia, please try to relax." So I didn't say anything at all. Besides, I was beginning to feel sorry for her. If she treated all her employees the way she treated her secretary—giving her work that was unrelated to her office duties, then taking the credit for the work done—I could easily understand some disgruntled coworker ordering twenty-five pizzas delivered to Ms. MacDonald, or putting her name on every junk-mail list available. But if what Ms. MacDonald's secretary found in her employer's credit history was true, this was either a case of deep-seated hatred from a disturbed mind bent on revenge, or Cynthia MacDonald was the victim of true name fraud.

"Okay, Cynthia. Do you have any idea of who might be doing this to you? Is someone out for revenge?"

She gave me an impatient sigh. "I can't think of anyone offhand. Although it doesn't happen very often, sometimes a client of mine has a setback due to some financial recommendation I made, but most of them are pretty gracious about the loss."

I slid a small legal pad and a pencil over to her. "Make a list of the ones who weren't very gracious about it." As an afterthought, I added, "In fact, make a list of all the clients who had financial setbacks up to the time your credit began to slip."

She stared at me. "You think this might be about revenge?"

I shrugged. "It's a possibility. The other possibility is that it's true name fraud. Tell me, was your wallet stolen at any time in the past, sometime around when this all began?"

"Yes, now that you mention it, my purse was stolen during rush hour on the Green line. I didn't even notice it was gone until I got off at Arlington Street."

"When did this happen?"

"About a month before my credit troubles began."

"Your credit cards were stolen, then," I said.

She nodded her head brusquely. "The police found my purse in a restaurant Dumpster off the Red line, at South Station, a few hours after I reported it stolen. It was minus the money and credit cards, but I reported the cards to the companies right away."

That didn't mean much, I thought. A lot of people didn't know that even if stolen credit cards were canceled, knowledgeable thieves could still use those same cards to establish credit.

I would have to check the police report and find out if my client was one of several purse snatchings, or was the only one. It wouldn't prove anything, but if she was the only one, it might point to Cynthia being a target. I steered my questions in that direction.

"What about your office? Is there anyone there you have some doubts about or that you find untrustworthy?"

She paused, then shook her head. "I trust everyone in the office implicitly."

She probably thought only of her colleagues—not the clerical staff.

I took another moment to think, then asked, "Including temp help and janitorial staff?" Most employers don't think about the temporary help as anything more than a convenience. Most employers didn't even think of temps in human terms, and they don't see temp help as a threat. I noticed she wasn't writing anything down yet—probably not used to taking her own dictation—so I decided to prod her. "While you're writing down this information, you might want to include the Tech City that you were in, and the name of the man you talked to."

"True name fraud," she said. She took out her Dayrunner and consulted it as she scribbled something down. "What do you know about it?" She put the pencil down, dug in her purse until she came up with a cigarette, then gave me an inquiring look.

I usually don't allow smoking in my office, but it was cool enough outside to open a window, and Cynthia MacDonald looked as if she really needed it. She lit up and looked around for an ashtray. I found an empty pop can in my wastebasket—slap me on the wrist for not recycling—and handed it to her. With a look of distaste, she took it.

"It's not a real familiar crime yet," I said. Lee Randolph, my police detective friend, and I had talked about it a couple of times. Lee told me that it was a hard crime to prove, and that quite often it was difficult to get a conviction even if the perp was picked up. "It's mostly a crime committed by rings of criminals working together. But I've been told that a person's identity is a valuable asset these days, and if your pocket is picked or your wallet is stolen on the subway, you may be out more than just the bucks you had on your person. The mugger can sell your identity to a credit-fraud ring and you can be taken for mucho more."

She grimaced. "I know more about that end of it now than I care to. But I still say I'm not paying for it. The credit companies should have caught on by now. I notified them the minute I discovered that someone was using my name and credit. And I filed a police report as well, but the police seem to be as much in the dark as I am."

I shrugged but didn't say anything. I wasn't going to argue with her. Lee had told me that victims of true name fraud could still be charged for the first fifty to one thousand dollars, depending on the credit-card company. As far as I was concerned, the apocalypse was just around the corner with the advent of "instant credit."

"So what exactly do you want me to do for you?"

"Find the sons of bitches who did this to me."
That was pretty clear. Cynthia tapped her cigarette
ash into the pop can. "I wanna sue the crap out of
them."

Something was bothering me and I had to know.
"But if you've already filed a police report, you
don't need me."

Cynthia gave me an impatient look. "I'm trying
to buy a house. It's not easy in this area for a single
woman to do, but it's impossible when you have to
deal with a messy credit record, even if a police
report backs you up." She tapped the file between
us. "Copies of the bills from the other Cynthia Mac-
Donald are in this folder, as well as copies of the
reports I filed, and letters from my lawyer to the
credit-card companies. I also included my own
credit record for comparison purposes." She handed
me the legal pad with a few names and phone numbers scribbled on it. "I'll have to fax the information
on coworkers who might dislike me, and the names
of temp agencies. Or better yet, you can talk to Amy
Brandywine, the personnel director at my broker-
age."

I studied the bills. They all had the same address,
an address that didn't match the one that Cynthia
MacDonald had given me as hers.

"I know what you're thinking," Cynthia said. "I
already went to that address and it was a mail drop.
There wasn't anyone to talk to." She went on to
explain that she had contacted the credit-card companies to stop the billing, and to tell them what had

happened. "In some cases, it took more than my Social Security card to convince them that I was the real Cynthia MacDonald. I wish they'd been as careful when my other self was applying for my credit," she added bitterly.

I had to sympathize with her—there's nothing like having an identity crisis. A $75,000 identity crisis. I asked her to at least write down the name and precinct of the policeman she had talked to. It would be a place to start.

We went over the standard contract, and after she had written out a check for a week of my time, my client got up to leave.

"I have to get to work. I took an hour off to come here and hire you." She extended her hand and I shook it. "I'll expect to hear from you in a few days. To report on your progress."

I nodded. "I'll see what I can do. I hope to have something for you by then."

She started to leave, then turned around. "Do you know how much of a violation this is?" she asked, her manner hesitant for the first time.

I looked straight into her eyes and saw the anger and fear there.

"It's as if…" She faltered, then continued, "…as if I'd been raped." There was a pause. "Does that seem weird?"

I shook my head. "No, it doesn't. Someone without a face or a name has taken over your identity, has messed with your good credit standing, and they had no right to do that. Just like in a rape case, the victim often gets the blame and there's no justice.''

Her jaw jutted out and her face turned grim. ''Well, I want justice. I don't care how I get it, but I want to teach whoever is doing this a lesson they won't forget. And I want to buy that damned house.''

TWO

I SPENT THE REST of the day on the phone, following up the bills she had left with me. Most of them were from "instant credit" stores, mostly electronics stores and clothing stores. Initially, there had been a flurry of "instant credit" activity; then it had begun to slow down before the false Cynthia started to widen her circle of credit destruction to Framingham, Rhode Island, and even to a store in Hartford, Connecticut. The false Cynthia hadn't been shy about spending money for five-star restaurants, designer clothing, gold and diamond jewelry, computers and other electronic equipment that could be returned for cash or hocked.

Most of the accounts with larger stores would be difficult, if not impossible, to follow up. It's hard to trace information about purchases through stores that employ more than ten people. I finally found a car-rental account called Sam's Car Lease & Rental in Revere that sounded promising. I made a note of the address and decided to just drop in. No point in putting anyone's guard up before I got a chance to talk to them in person.

I locked up my office and walked to the parking garage where I keep my car. I'd recently rented a space there near my North End office for those winter days when I didn't feel like taking the T. The space, of course, was courtesy of one of my shirttail relatives, all of whom Ma uses as her own personal discount Yellow Pages.

I'd traded in my Corsica for an older, more reliable car. Actually, I'd liked the Corsica, but my heart was set on a sport-utility vehicle. I'd wanted a Jeep Grand Cherokee but, silly me, I didn't have twenty-three grand to spend and Ma sent me to an uncle of hers who owns a used-car lot out in Mattapan. Uncle Vito offered me a nice used '92 Bronco for about half the price, so I went with it. It even came with an engine heater for those below-zero nights.

It was midafternoon when I hopped into my car, started that puppy up, and drove out to Revere, where Sam's Car Lease & Rental was located on a low-rent, secondhand auto row where dealerships sprang up one day and were gone the next day.

It almost surprised me to find the place still there. Inside, the woman behind the desk looked like someone's grandmother instead of the usual eighteen-year-old with the brains of a clam. This woman with iron-gray curls beamed at me when I walked through the door. The place was just big enough to accommodate the employee and a customer. There was no high-tech equipment—no computers, not even an electronic typewriter. There were file cabinets behind the counter, and lots of paper and pens. While I was surveying the place, I spied a photocopier out of the corner of my eye, and had to amend my first impression.

"What can I do for you, dearie?" she asked as she scribbled something down on a car-rental form. Her name tag read "Bernice."

I leaned against the battered linoleum counter. I hadn't thought about how I wanted to handle this—should I tell the truth or make up a story? Merchant reactions vary from apathy to concern when it comes to true name fraud. I decided to opt for a half-truth.

"Hi, Bernice," I said with my best disarming grin. "I was wondering if you could help me with a little problem. You see, my sister leased or rented a car from you a few weeks ago and the family hasn't heard from her since then. She just disappeared." I worked up a tragic and earnest expression.

She frowned and tapped her pen against the form. "Oh, you poor dear. Little ones?"

"Pardon me?" I asked.

"Does she have children?" Bernice repeated patiently.

"Oh, well, yes. Two." I thought about it and patted my stomach. "Well, three. One on the way. Little Derek, Lindsey, and...well, she doesn't know what the other one is yet."

"You can get tested to find out. Ultra-something-or-other. It's not real reliable, but it gives you a better idea."

"Sound. It's called ultrasound. And Cynthia isn't

far enough along to find out whether it's a boy or a girl." I got a faraway look in my eyes.

"Oh, dear. Hormones?" she asked.

"I'm not married."

"No, I mean your sister Cynthia. Hormones. Is that why she ran away? Hormones can run rampant when you get pregnant. Having children takes its toll." She nodded wisely. Obviously, this was a woman who had had the experience of children and they had taken their toll on her. I pictured little cartoon hormones running wildly around in circles, sort of like what I was doing at the moment.

I didn't think hormones had anything to do with my bogus sister's running away. "Uh, I don't think she ran away. See"—I had to think fast—"I think it was the husband. Ronald." Ronald MacDonald? Where did I come up with these ideas? "I think he might have something to do with her disappearance. It was an unhappy marriage."

She'd started looking in her files. "Name?"

"Matelli."

"Ronald and Cynthia Matelli."

"No," I said quickly. "Her name is MacDonald. Cynthia MacDonald."

"And Ronald MacDonald?" Bernice looked at me over her eyeglasses, and I could see that for the first time she was beginning to doubt the validity of my story.

I shrugged helplessly. "What can I say? His parents had a sense of humor." I decided it wasn't a good time to go into a big deal about Ronald being born in a McDonald's near the fries section. That would probably be too much.

This story was costing me more time than it was worth. And I was really getting into the idea that I had a sister named Cynthia who was missing, and her kids were worried, and her husband might or might not be involved in foul play.

Bernice pulled a card, then walked over to the dull-gray metal file cabinets, slid open a drawer, and took a thin file out. As she came back to the counter, she paused and looked around in a secretive manner before shooting a coy look in my direction. "I really shouldn't be giving you this information. For all I know, you're a cop or something."

Like that would be bad. But then again, I had a feeling that business practices at this dealership probably weren't on the up-and-up.

"Ma'am, if I were a cop, I would have pulled a badge."

Bernice still hesitated. "Well, I might get in trouble for showing this information to you. Maybe she isn't missing after all. Maybe she's left him and the kids."

I pulled a twenty from my purse and pushed it across the counter. "Bernice, this is for the trouble you may have with your boss." Who was probably her grandson, I thought. One of the products of those little hormones running around rampantly.

She pursed her wrinkled lips into a half-smile and took the money discreetly before sliding the file over the counter. I half-expected her to tuck the bill in her bra, but she pocketed it casually, like she did this all the time.

As I scanned the file, I thanked the technology gods that this place hadn't gone computer-crazy yet. Sometimes the old-fashioned way is easier to work around.

I looked over the application and found the mail drop filled in on the address line, plus what I took to be a phony phone number. I made a few notes, then flipped the sheet over—there was a photocopy of a driver's license, complete with a bad picture. It wasn't a very good photocopy, but it would do. Bernice let me use the copy machine—free of charge, I might add. What came out of the machine was an almost unrecognizable copy of the driver's license.

I was trying to find an opportune moment when Bernice was distracted to pull a switch on the photocopies when the phone rang. While the morally bankrupt little old lady answered the call, I slipped the photocopy of the photocopy in the file. I figured the good photocopy was probably included in the price of Bernice's complicity.

"I hope you find her," she called out as I opened the door.

I waved the papers at her in a reassuring manner and smiled. "So do I."

But we weren't talking about the same Cynthia MacDonald.

ON MY WAY back to the office, I drove by the mail drop. It was a nondescript red-brick building on a shabby back street of Kenmore Square. I double-parked and jogged into the building. There was a door to the left of the mail boxes and I knocked and walked in. A young black woman was seated at a desk in the small office.

I introduced myself and explained the situation to her.

"I'd like to help you," she smiled sympathetically, "but these mail drops are private."

I smiled back. "I understand your dilemma, but I have to point out that I could go to the police with this information, and then your mail drop might lose some customers with the ensuing media coverage." I was counting on this woman being reluctant to let the police take a close interest in her establishment. Some of her customers were probably not on the up-and-up, and were paying for the privilege of keeping their business private.

She held my gaze for a few moments, then sighed. "What's the box number?"

I gave her the number. She looked it up on her computer. "That client dropped the box a few weeks ago."

I looked over the information she gave me, but it was clearly a dead end, and she knew it. I could see the relief in her eyes.

Still, I thanked her for cooperating and left. It had been too easy, and I knew it. If the box was still being rented, I could have staked out the building and caught the woman who was using my client's name and credit. But nothing is that simple.

Back at the office, I leaned carefully back in my chair and stared at the photograph again. The woman in it was far from the Cynthia MacDonald I'd met earlier in the day. She was much thinner than my client, and much better-looking. Her hair was nicely styled, and she was wearing what looked like good jewelry. All in all, if you didn't look too closely at the bleak expression in her eyes, she had the appearance of a well-off, upscale working woman. I had no idea of the color of her hair from the black-and-white copy of the license. The photograph was my only lead, so I would start with the two most direct approaches—I'd show the photo to Cynthia and to my Homicide detective friend, Lee Randolph.

I called Lee's office and left a message on his voice mail to call me tomorrow morning. Then, glancing at my watch, I thought about dropping by Cynthia's work, but I had aikido in about an hour. Considering how long it took her to hire me, I wasn't about to go trotting off to my client's office during rush hour only to have her drone on about her woes. I settled for calling her at the office to report my progress and to schedule a meeting for tomorrow.

"What do you have for me?" my client asked over the phone.

I gave her a short rundown of my day. "Look," I said when I'd finished, "I'd like to know if I could come down to your office in the morning to show you this photo."

"Why would I know this woman? Didn't you tell me chances are that this is a ring of some kind?" She paused, then said, "I'm looking at my Dayrunner, and I have meetings all day tomorrow. The day after would be better for me."

I mentally scrapped my plans to go to aikido. I'd sacrifice in order to get this case over with quickly. "How about tonight? Do you have any time tonight?"

"Mmmmm, I have a business dinner in half an hour. Some clients have flown in from Tokyo." I heard the speakerphone go on. Her voice sounded tinny and dismissive. "Besides, why do I need to see the photo? It's probably just some welfare mother who's making a few bucks with a credit-scam ring. I probably won't know her."

"I'm working on the process of elimination. If it's someone who knows you and this is a revenge motive, I don't want to waste your money or my time going through other possibilities. She may have worked in your office. She may have taken a credit application from you. She may clean your apartment."

I struck a nerve on that last one. "Lupe came highly recommended to me and has been working for me for the last two years," my client said. But beneath her indignant manner, I sensed that she was having trouble convincing herself.

I kept pressing the big red paranoid button. "If

this is an isolated crime, a case of someone who saw an opportunity and took it, I want to make sure I'm not running up your bill by going off on a wild-goose chase.'' I didn't mention that I was taking the photo to my friend on the force. I'd save that for later, if any information turned up.

I heard a beleaguered sigh on the other end. Cynthia MacDonald was a woman who liked to call the shots, and she probably was beginning to regret working with a wild card like me, but any good private investigator wouldn't let a client set the terms.

''All right. I can give you five minutes tomorrow at noon. And while you're here, you might want to talk to my personnel director, Amy Brandywine. She has a better memory for faces. And she works closely with the temp agencies.''

I made a note that I'd be talking to Ms. Brandy-wine.

''I got another credit report today and apparently I went in last month to a electronics store in Methuen. The only thing I'm grateful for is that she didn't spend up to the limit.''

''Ouch. Have you taken care of it?''

''I called the policeman I've been dealing with and gave him the news.''

I thought about it. ''Give me the name of the store to add to my list. The information I requested earlier today, you can give that to me tomorrow when I come in.''

I thanked her and hung up, wondering how Amy

Brandywine was going to react to the news that I would be taking up part of her lunch hour. I was sure that I'd be popular with her.

A glance at my watch made me realize I had to hustle to get to my class. I picked up my gym bag and locked up the office.

WHEN I GOT TO the dojo, it was nice to hang around with the guys. Recently, several women had joined, and I had mixed feelings about it. I liked being the only woman in the dojo on one hand, but on the other hand, I didn't want to be a prima donna and so I went out of my way to be nice to Anna and Christy. They were a lesbian couple who had decided that they wanted to do some form of exercise together.

Anna used to be a black belt in karate, but her last instructor didn't like to have women in his class and made no attempt to disguise his bias. She quit in disgust. Anna's lover, Christy, was ex-Navy. She had the coolest Popeye tattoo on her forearm. She told me her ship had been docked in San Diego and she'd been out drinking with some shipmates. I guess that's how most servicemen and women get their tattoos. I was one of the few marines who hadn't gotten a tattoo. Most of the women in my unit had gotten one, but I just couldn't see myself with a tattoo on my ass of a baby devil in a diaper.

Dave ran us through our warm-ups, then we began to work out. I usually begin to lose interest in a sport after a few months, but I'd been pretty faithful to aikido. I'd tried boxing for a while when it was popular a few years ago, and although it was a good workout, I got bored with it. There's a rhythm to it, and after I missed the rhythm and got socked in the face for the umpteenth time and broke my nose, I gave it up. I'm not Cindy Crawford beautiful but I'm not bad-looking, and didn't want to mess up the parts of my face that were still in place.

After class, I talked to Dave. "How's the move coming along?"

He grimaced. "I think we're ready to move sometime this coming weekend. You free?"

My sister Sophia, my friend Dave, and her kids were moving in together. He had obtained his divorce papers and Sophia had cleaned up her act. Sophia and I had always had a prickly relationship because Sophia tended to take advantage of me, usually through Ma.

Sophia and I were getting along better these days. She often told me I had mellowed, but I doubted that. It must have had something to do with the fact that she was in love with a nice guy, for a change. As long as she was happy, she was nicer to me than she'd been in a long time.

I grinned. "Sure. I may be losing a tenant, but I'm gaining…" I trailed off and put on a puzzled look. "Hey, I'm just losing a tenant, right? What am I gaining?"

Dave suppressed a smile. "Some peace and quiet."

"Yeah, but I'm gonna miss the lasagna." Sophia

makes the best lasagna in the world. Lately she had become very domestic, helping Ma with Sunday dinner and learning how to cook more of Ma's fabulous dishes. Dave was impressed enough to move in with her. Dave, in the meantime, has become Ma's favorite. Even Ma realizes—although she will deny it to her grave—that Sophia had made bad choices when it came to men. Ma always pats Dave's cheek and says what a good boy her Sophia is marrying—though, of course, no one ever brings up marriage except Ma.

Sophia and Dave have been living in sin, which is fine with me. They've found a great apartment in Brookline, near his work, and Sophia has given up her job at the bar and is taking night courses in nursing. The idea of Sophia nursing anyone back to health often sends me into gales of laughter, but then, I'm sure I'm not her idea of a private investigator, either. Sophia's kids, Stephanie and Michael, are getting a real dad for a change, a role model who doesn't drink in excess, ride a Harley, and who doesn't think a night isn't complete unless he's been in at least one bar fight.

Dave broke into my thoughts. "I talked to Rosa the other day and she told me she was sticking with the art history major."

I nodded. Rosa had gone through a major crisis— pun intended—just a year ago. She'd decided that archaeology wasn't for her, and after spending a few hours in jail because she'd botched a job for me, Rosa decided that art history was a better major for her. Since then, she'd gotten an internship at the Boston Museum of Fine Arts, and three days a week she conducts tours for grade-school field trips and groups of tourists. She's really gotten good at it, especially explaining art to school kids, and finds that she has a great interest in the Old Masters. She also has a good eye for art and has started collecting folk art for her apartment.

On occasion, Rosa still works for me. When I get behind on insurance investigation assignments, or when I have a case that takes more time, she'll help me catch up. The only thing she won't touch is repos because she feels that the people who got behind in their payments on cars or washing machines are just poor working schlubs. No matter how many times I've tried to explain it to her, I can't make her see that not every person whose car or TV has to be repossessed has good intentions and no money. Even then, it didn't make it right. The companies who pay me to repo a car are losing money and, in turn, the average customer ends up paying more for a car. In my opinion, right and wrong don't enter into the equation.

I said goodnight to the other students, took a raincheck on an invitation to join Anna and Christy for an after-aikido nosh, and headed for my car. Driving home, I thought about tomorrow's moves. I'd already run down the one lead that looked good. I still had the picture of the woman who was passing herself off as my client and I knew I had to show the copy of the photo to Cynthia MacDonald to get her reaction. I hoped that if my client saw the face, it might jar loose some memory.

When I got home, I fed my pet iguana, Fredd. I'd decided to try a pet, but I didn't want a cat or a dog. Too much work, too much litter to clean up. Fish mean having to clean a messy bowl or an aquarium, and that's too much of a commitment for me. So I got myself Fredd. He's bright green, has wizened eyes, and sits on a branch in a dry aquarium. Nice and neat. All I have to do is clean out the wood shavings in his aquarium every few days, keep his water fresh, feed him alfalfa pellets, fruit and vegetables, and the occasional housefly, and he's happy. And so am I.

Friends ask me all the time why I named him Fredd. I just reply that he looks sort of like Fred Mertz on *I Love Lucy*. Then they give me this strange look. But I've grown fond of old Fredd. I know there's something wrong with me when I start thinking about bringing him to my office as a watch iguana.

I had finally broken down and bought an answering machine for my home a couple of months ago. I saw there was one message blinking on it, so I pressed the playback.

"Angela, this is your mother calling. I have some good news. Call me when you get home."

I reached for the phone and, wondering what the good news was, punched in Ma's number. "Hi, Ma, it's me." Ma knows each of us by the sound of our voices. I think we all sound alike, but she zeroes in on the little differences. "What's the good news?"

"Angie! I'm so glad you called. I've got it all set up."

"Set up what?"

"Well, you see, my dear sister Emily Giordano's son has just graduated from medical school. He's taken a job with Brigham and Women's and, well, he doesn't know the city too well. I thought maybe you could show him around."

Uh-huh. This was Ma's subtle way of getting me to go on a blind date. I told her as much. "How can you even think that?" she asked me in a hurt tone. "Emily was one of my best friends at the sorority, and I thought it would be the least you could do for one of my friends."

I'd never heard of Emily until this moment, so I highly doubted that they were best friends. Probably passing acquaintances who realized their children weren't married yet, and they thought they'd try matching us up. Besides, what was the deal with me showing her sorority sister's son a good time? The least *I* could do? I thought not. But haggling with Ma always wears me down, and I finally agreed to see him.

"Oh, that's good. He'll be waiting for you at Sablone's tomorrow night at seven."

"Ma—"

"Oh, you don't know how grateful Emily is that you're doing this."

"But—"

"His name is Reginald."

I gave up trying to protest and said good-bye to a very smug Ma. She had finally gotten me a date with a doctor. Oh, she might couch it in terms of "showing him around the city" and "making him feel at home," but if that were really the case, she wouldn't have set up this first meeting as a dinner date. It's hard to show anyone the city at seven at night when you're sitting in Sablone's, which has excellent veal but not much of a view, unless you like a cozy table in a dark corner.

Reginald. I knew I shouldn't jump to conclusions about a man I don't know, based just on his name, but "Reginald" was so British. Stiff, formal. Sir Reginald. Reggie. I wondered what his idea of a night out on the town was like—tea and crumpets with the queen?

On the other hand, "Reginald" made me think "rich." This guy could be wealthy. Hey, he's a doctor. Even if he's not rich now, he will be soon. Maybe this blind date wouldn't turn out so bad after all.

Yeah, this was going to be fun.

THREE

THE NEXT MORNING I tried to figure out what to wear. Normally, it's not a problem. I usually show up at my office in jeans and whatever shirt is hanging in my closet, but I knew I had to make a good impression at my client's office.

Most of my shirts come from Rosa, Sophia, or various relatives. Sometimes I stop by Filene's basement or Hit or Miss for a sale, and sometimes I shop at Goodwill and Salvation Army. I hate paying full price for anything. One of my weirdest purchases was a black Benetton blouse in a heavy rayon for fifteen bucks at an antique shop. My closest friend, Raina, loves to go antiquing, and sometimes I'm forced to go with her. When we found this retro swing blouse, she insisted that I buy it. "It's you," she kept telling me.

I personally didn't think I looked all that good in it, but it's turned out to be a great basic to wear with either jeans or a skirt. So I decided to wear it with a pair of black jeans.

My taste in clothes is getting better, mostly because I rely on my friends, who have better taste than I. When they aren't around and I'm looking through my closets, I go by one special rule: I can't go wrong with basic black. My second rule is that neutral colors work together, and my third rule is that if I do wear a bright or pastel blouse or skirt, something white or black must always accompany it. This way, I keep myself from looking like a clown. Sometimes I miss the order that comes with military life. In the Marines, I never had to think about what to wear every morning when I woke up. Even on my days off, I wore jeans and a T-shirt or an L.L. Bean cotton-flannel or chambray shirt. I didn't have to work all that hard at getting myself together.

After I got dressed, I looked at myself in the mirror and was pleased with the result. The sunglasses clinched the casual rock-star look. I could see myself being photographed in an airport on my way to Milan, bottled Naya water in hand.

I took the T to Haymarket and walked to my office in the North End, stopping along the way to get an egg, mozzarella, and roasted red-pepper sandwich on an English muffin at Max's Deli Cafe on Milk Street. I'm a regular customer, so the cook always adds a couple of extra peppers. The accompanying fried new potatoes are delicious and probably very fattening, but I work out enough to afford them occasionally.

I spent the morning following up on some of the credit-card bills and checking on the electronics store that had recently given instant credit to my client without her knowledge. The store was called "Technology Bytes," and was located in Methuen, near the New Hampshire border.

I called and talked to Mr. Clemens, the store manager. He didn't sound surprised to hear about the credit fraud.

"It's happening everywhere these days," he said with a sigh. "Even here in a small place like Methuen. The credit-card scammers are moving out of the big cities, as far away from their home base as possible, so we have a hard time catching them."

I asked him about the case in question: "It's been a few weeks, but since you are in a small town, is it possible that your salesperson would remember the transaction, maybe be able to identify the photo I have?"

"Sure, bring it up to the store. It can't hurt to see if one of us remembers." It sounded like a small place. Maybe there was hope after all. I checked the date of the sale against when the car had been rented, and they matched. This was starting to look as if it was going somewhere. I made sure Mr. Clemens would be in the store tomorrow afternoon, then hung up.

About ten minutes to noon, I walked over to my client's office, which was only a few blocks from mine. She worked for an investment company at 100 Federal Street, an imposing red-granite building that looked as though the contractor had built it upside down. The lobby was marble—real marble, to my uneducated eye—and it was hard to find the directory. I finally found it discreetly hidden in these built-in black marble "sculptures" against the walls. Cynthia worked for Tremaine, Farquhar, and Pennyworth Investments. I couldn't believe there was a real Pennyworth—they had to have made it up to impart some sort of psychological security to their clients. The investment firm seemed to be in good company, though—all the best investment companies were housed in this building.

I took the elevator to the fifteenth floor and walked down the hushed corridor—with its lush carpeting and wall sconces that shed a soothing, subtle light; this wasn't a hall, it was a corridor that only rich and powerful people strode down. I came to the thick glass door, which had a security lock. Through the door I could see the receptionist punching buttons and talking into the little headset that seemed to be growing out of her ear. Several men came into the lobby out of a corner office. Their Gucci shoes and Perry Ellis suits gave them away—they were the owners of the investment firm, not the brokers. I watched the receptionist hurriedly glance up at them, then turn away.

As the men left the office, they didn't seem to notice me slip inside. If they had, they probably would have thought I was delivering a sandwich to one of the overworked and underpaid employees who labored through their lunch hour. Once inside, I took a corner chair in the lobby and waited for the receptionist to take a breather. It was a good ten minutes before she noticed my presence. She jumped slightly, then relaxed.

"Are you waiting for someone?" The implication

was that I obviously wasn't a client, so I must be waiting for a friend who worked here.

"Cynthia MacDonald, please."

With a touch of a computer key, she referred to Cynthia's schedule and frowned. "I don't see any appointment for noon with Ms. MacDonald. Are you sure you have the date right?"

"Just call her. She'll see me. Tell her Angela Matelli's waiting."

The receptionist looked doubtful, but she got through to my client, who apparently chewed her out for not sending me in sooner. I was given directions to my client's office three doors down on the right of the left-hand corridor. Cynthia MacDonald's door was ajar, and she was organizing her briefcase. Her hair was swept up in a chignon and she wore a black pantsuit today, paired with an ivory silk shell. Gold earrings completed the starkly elegant ensemble.

I showed her the photocopy. She studied it seriously, then shook her head. "I honestly can't recall her. It's not a very good picture, is it?"

I shrugged. "It's what I have to work with."

She seemed distracted. I reminded her about the notes she was supposed to have written up.

She brightened momentarily. "Oh, yes. I had my secretary enter them and print it out." She touched a button. "Mona? Are you still there?" She paused, waiting, but her servant had actually gone to lunch. Looking ever so slightly annoyed, Cynthia bustled out the door and came back a moment later with a couple of sheets of paper stapled together. She handed them to me. "Here they are. Mona's usually so reliable." I refrained from pointing out that Mona had done the work. The fact that it hadn't traveled from Mona's desk to hers wasn't a big deal, but I supposed that in my client's business world, it probably was.

Looking around her office one more time, she picked up her briefcase. "Well, I have an important meeting in New York." Opening a closet door, Cynthia pulled out a small carry-on with built-in wheels. An airline ticket peeked out from a side pocket in the coat that was draped over the suitcase. "I'll be back tomorrow afternoon if you have anything more to report."

"That's fine. You mentioned Amy Brandywine. Is she still in?"

Cynthia rolled her eyes. "She hardly ever leaves her desk. Let me call her." A moment later, I was ushered out of my client's office and taken down the corridor, turning left and left again. A young, frizzyhaired blond sat behind her desk, a sandwich in front of her, a bottle of juice in her hand.

The woman blinked and looked in my direction. "Oh, yes, Ms. Matelli." She looked around as if she wasn't sure of what to do first—offer me a seat or clean up her desk. She finally settled for sweeping the half-eaten sandwich off her desk first, then got up and extended her hand. "I'm terribly sorry. I thought you'd be longer with Ms. MacDonald."

"I'm sorry to disturb your lunch hour."

Cynthia stood behind me. She waved her hand. "Amy always eats here. We can't get her to leave the office for an hour's break." She glanced at her watch. "My limo should be waiting outside by now. If anything develops, please leave a message here at the office, and also on my answering machine at home."

I refrained from saluting as my client turned and left.

Ms. Brandywine offered me a seat. I noted the office window overlooked Fanueil Hall. It was odd that someone of her status in the company should have an office with a view. The way Cynthia had spoken of her was dismissive, the way a boss speaks about an employee. Amy Brandywine followed my admiring gaze.

"My father owns the company."

I looked at her in surprise. An admission like that was commendable.

She smiled. "But I proved myself at another, larger investment firm before taking a job here. Once the other company offered me the same position, I came to my father and negotiated with him."

I raised my eyebrows. My admiration for this woman grew. I thought about the name of the firm. "Is Brandywine your married name?" It was a sexist question, but she shrugged, taking it in stride. I've never been known for my political correctness.

"No, my father's Arthur Tremaine. I took my mother's maiden name just to keep the inevitable questions at bay.'' Then she got down to business. ''I understand that you have a picture of a woman you want to have identified.''

I showed her the photo. She looked at it carefully before handing it back. ''It's not a real good copy, but it could be someone who worked here as a temp. I know she didn't work here as a full-time employee—I have a good memory for faces if they stay around long enough. But if she worked here for only a few days, I wouldn't remember her. I'm sorry I can't be of more help. I wish it had been instant recognition. If I can help you in any other way—''

''Actually, can you give me the name of the temp agency you use? I can show this picture around and maybe someone will recognize her.''

She frowned. ''I use two temp agencies. But I have to say, it sounds like a long shot.''

I thanked her while she wrote down the names of the agencies, the contact names, and the numbers.

''I don't suppose you have a photo of the real Ms. MacDonald, do you?''

She looked up and nodded. ''We have photos for the employee badges. Duplicates are kept in the file.'' She handed me the memo note with the temp agencies' names on it, got up and went through her file cabinets. I was really beginning to think file cabinets are the wave of the future. You can access them easily, and they never crash on you.

A moment later, Amy Brandywine handed me a fairly recent photo of Cynthia, who looked as if having her picture taken was equal to being on death row. I couldn't help but smile. Amy chuckled. "She's not the easiest person to capture on film." She closed her eyes and grimaced. "I'm sorry. That was cruel."

I shrugged. "I always look like a troll on camera. You probably take a pretty good picture."

She picked up the photocopy again and studied it, shaking her head. "I guess I do. This woman *does* look familiar. I wish I could remember where I've seen her before."

"If it helps at all, she would have to have worked here right before Ms. MacDonald's financial troubles began," I pointed out.

"That would have been about three months ago, right?"

"Well," I hedged, "actually, it can take up to two to three months for this stuff to show up in your record, sometimes up to six months. It all depends on how quickly the credit companies begin suspecting anything, and how willing they are to do anything about it."

She turned back to her computer and consulted her records. Finally, she shook her head. "No. We didn't use any temps back in March. No one in the clerical staff was out sick that month, and everyone was trying to catch up on the work that didn't get done over the holidays. Sorry."

I thanked her and stood up. "I have another appointment, and I've taken up quite a bit of your lunch hour. Thanks for your time."

We shook hands and she made me promise to let her know if I identified the woman in the photo.

FOUR

MY NEXT STOP was to see Lee at the Berkeley Street precinct. I'd had a message from him asking me to stop by in the early afternoon, and one o'clock seemed early enough. He'd just gotten back from lunch. I hadn't taken the time to stop and eat. I reminded myself that eating wasn't the most important thing in life, but my stomach kept growling. Lee noticed when I settled into the chair reserved for special visitors.

"Hey, Matelli, I had a nice big sub for lunch. Lots of steak and Swiss cheese, peppers and onions—"

"Shut up, Lee, and take a look at this. Can you run it through Vice?"

He took the photocopy that I offered him. After a moment, he asked what it was all about. I told him.

"Talk about finding a needle in a haystack, Matelli. But hey, if anyone can do it, you can. How am I supposed to run it through Vice on just a picture? The Vice guys don't have the kind of time that'd require going through the books."

"But this is what I get paid to do," I said. "If you could give me access to the books, that's all I ask."

Lee picked up the phone and called down to the

department. I was in luck. The books weren't in use. While we waited for someone to deliver them, I asked, "How long do you think this will take?"

He thought. "Probably not long. There aren't as many books on female offenders."

"If I do find out who this is," I replied in a morose tone, "it'll be sheer dumb luck."

"You got plenty of that, all right."

It took me a good two hours to go through the books of female offenders. Several times I thought I had a match, but once it turned out the woman was dead and had been for almost a year, and another time it turned out the offender was in prison for fifteen years and there was no way she was getting out. Toward the end, all of the faces in the books were starting to look a little like my mystery woman.

I was beginning to wonder if this had been such a good idea, but I had to check out the possibilities. When I flipped the last page of the last book, I was disappointed to find out I wasn't a beneficiary of sheer dumb luck, or even of a mild coincidence. The face in the photograph wasn't there, and if she had a record, it wasn't enough to get her in the Sears catalog of female offenders. Maybe she had a traffic ticket. I didn't think the Traffic Department took pictures of violators.

I thanked Lee and promised to make dinner for him next week. He reminded me about the poker game coming up, and then I left the station.

I CONSULTED THE FILE that Cynthia had given me. Tech City in Quincy would be a fairly easy drive.

In fact, I'd be driving against rush hour traffic if I made the appointment for midafternoon.

I called the Tech City in Quincy and got an adenoidal teenager on the phone who didn't seem to want to do anything that would require using his head.

"What's this about?" he asked for the third time.

"I'm calling about checking on someone's credit at your store."

"We don't give out that information over the phone."

I'd just gone over this with him, and I was about at the end of my patience. "I understand that. I want to know the location of your regional office."

There was a pause, then he seemed to be consulting with someone else, then he came back. "Ma'am? Let me put you on hold and try to get a number."

And he put me on hold—for the third time. I was about ready to scream and hang up when he came back on the line. "Ma'am? You'd talk to Mr. Balczeck." There was another pause. "He's with the regional office, but he works out of an office here sometimes."

"Would you please connect me?" I asked as politely as possible through gritted teeth.

"Uh, yeah, sure." There was a click, then it rang through. At least the guy got something right. I'd expected to be cut off.

"Balczeck here."

He sounded no nonsense, so I got right to it, introducing myself and asking for an appointment.

"Sure, you can come in any time except noon to one, my lunch hour. Maybe you can tell me what this is about so I have an idea—" He left the rest of the sentence unfinished, waiting for me to fill him in.

I'd considered being straight with him, but I decided some mystery was in order. I didn't want him to cut me off or question who I was and how I was involved with Cynthia MacDonald's credit. At least, not until I met him face to face. It was easier to put someone off if you didn't have to put a face to a name.

"I'd rather lay it all out for you when I get there," I said. "It's a credit problem."

"Okay," he replied. We agreed on three o'clock and I hung up.

This was the store that had turned Cynthia down for credit, the place where she discovered that she had an alternate personality. Tech City was a large chain that seemed to have sprung up overnight. The Quincy store was off Route 93, a freeway I hate to drive on—it's crowded and there's always construction on the roads. As far as I knew from seeing my client's list of credit cards and purchases, she rarely went anywhere that wasn't within Boston proper.

I got to Tech City at three in the afternoon. Even on a weekday in the dead of the afternoon, there were crowds of people swarming over the store, taking advantage of the supposed "special deals" that some adenoidal teenager was announcing over the loudspeaker. Whoever dreamed up Tech City must have done his thesis on how Kmart works. He had even stolen the "blue-light special" idea.

I passed the announcer. He wasn't a teen—he was about thirty years old, with frown lines on his forehead. Probably permanently pissed off that he'd never gone through the voice change. He wasn't bad-looking, in a Squiggy type of way, and I could see some women going for him. Me, I thought he was the type of guy who always had to "prove" himself; after all, he was working in this second-rate discount electronics store. I suppose I'd be pissed off, too. His store ID badge told me his name was Jimmy.

He was all smiles when I first asked for the manager. Mr. Balczeck.

"You have an appointment?" he asked, quivering in his tacky, bright green sales jacket.

I nodded. "I talked to him earlier. He told me he'd be here." I handed my business card to him.

He studied the card, then looked up at me with wide eyes. "You looking for a job here?"

I sometimes get these curiosity seekers. They can't just follow a simple request, they have to make your job harder. I made a point of looking at my watch, then crossed my arms. "I'd like to see Mr. Balczeck, please."

He wavered for a moment, then told me to follow him. We went through a set of swinging doors marked "Employees Only" and stopped at the first door on the right. It was a small office, but outfitted with a computer, a television, a VCR, and everything else that was state of the art. Of course, since this was a discount electronics store, I expected that middle- and higher-management types would get perks like this in their offices. The lowly employees, I suspected, just got the standard employee discount—usually thirty percent—on items they wanted.

Mr. Balczeck sat behind his desk and stood when I entered the room. He shook my hand and offered me a seat. He was a large, comfortable-looking man. His hair had migrated from the top of his head to growing out of his ears and between his eyebrows, but he had a pleasant face.

"What can I do for you, Ms.—" he consulted the business card I'd handed to him when I first came in the door "—Matelli?"

Jimmy hesitated in the doorway. "I think she wants to apply for a job as store detective, Mr. Balczeck." He shot me a look that I took to mean that he sort of wanted that position for himself. The manager looked up from my card and waved him away.

"It's okay, Jimmy. I know what she wants, and it isn't a job. Why don't you go back to the floor and help some customers." He consulted a couple of security monitors that were mounted in a corner of the room. Each gave a different view of the store. "I see that we're short of help again today."

I glanced at one of the monitors and noted that a teenager in the CD section was slipping a disc into one of his long pockets. "Do you get a lot of that?" I pointed to the monitor where the kid was obliging me by looking furtively around before slipping a second CD into his pocket.

Balczeck nodded to Jimmy. "Better check that one out. Give him a chance to return the merchandise before he leaves the store."

Jimmy hurried out of the office and I was alone with Mr. Balczeck. I went over the reason for our meeting.

When I finished, he took up a pen and started making notes. "Okay, so you're saying that this woman, Cynthia MacDonald, came in to this store on what day?"

I consulted my file. "Saturday, the twelfth."

He scribbled something down. "And she applied for instant credit because she wanted to buy a big-screen television. And she was turned down because someone had already used her name at another store." He looked up at me. "I don't mean to sound like I'm telling you how to do your job, but could this be a mix-up?"

I smiled and shook my head. "She's already filed a report with the police in Boston. Someone's using her name for this credit-card scam. I'm investigating it, trying to determine if this is just one person, or if it's part of a ring."

He shook his head with a smile. "I sure don't know how you're going to figure this one out. We've had a few of these problems here over the years, and it's always hard to find the person or persons behind them. Even if we suspect something, they usually have good instincts and they're out of here before the police arrive in time for the arrest.''

"Sounds like you've had a few professional rings scam you in the past," I said.

He leaned back in his chair. "So tell me, why did you stop by here? I'm not sure I can be of much help beyond swapping stories of scam artists."

I shrugged and smiled. "I'm covering all bases."

"I'm curious," Balczeck said, leaning forward and folding his hands. "Have you found a lead?"

I showed him the photo of the fake Cynthia MacDonald and explained how I got it. He studied the picture with a frown. In fact, he stared at it for such a long time that I couldn't tell if he was memorizing her face or if something was wrong.

"Does she look familiar?" I finally asked.

He looked up at me and smiled in a distracted manner. Glancing up at the monitors, he said, "I just wanted to make sure I would recognize her face if she came in the store. Do you mind if I make a copy of this and keep it here? I could show it around to the employees. I'm not always here, you know." He studied me for a moment, then sat forward in his chair and typed in a few keystrokes on his computer. "Tell you what I'm gonna do. I'll look up that name for you and tell you what's going on from our end."

"That'd be great," I replied.

A few moments later, Balczeck leaned back in his chair. "It says here that Cynthia MacDonald," with a wry grin, he added, "the person who used Ms.

MacDonald's credit, opened up an account in the Mattapan branch store last March."

I started to rise. "I guess I should pursue that angle. Thanks for looking that information up for me."

He gestured for me to sit down and turned back to me. "I'm afraid Mattapan won't do you much good. We've had a major turnover there recently. I'm embarrassed to admit it, but the employees walked out on us because of the way management was treating them."

I blinked. "Really? Why strike in only the one store?"

He shrugged. "It was the manager, a real power-hungry sort. She couldn't handle the stress. Didn't know how to treat people, and by the time we got to the employees, ninety percent of them had found other jobs. The other ten percent were kicked upstairs or moved on to other stores. Hard to track them at this point."

"Oh. Well, thanks for telling me."

"I'll look in the employee files for you, but I don't think it would do much good. Most people aren't going to remember someone they sold something to four, five, six months ago."

"Thanks for the offer, anyway," I replied, knowing it was a perfunctory offer. He wasn't really going to nose into all those employee files, he was just trying to make her feel as if something was going to be done about a woman whose credit history had been ruined.

"Anyway, let me make that xerox."

I nodded, but knew it was a long shot. Still, I appreciated the fact that this guy wanted to cooperate.

As he copied the photo on the personal copier that sat in a corner of the office, he turned to me and smiled again. "Who knows? Maybe we'll get lucky. I have your card, I can contact you. Do you have any other questions?"

"Tell me something," I said. "If you work in the regional office, why do you have an office here?"

He smiled. "You're lucky to catch me here. I come in twice a week at the most. I live in Quincy, and it's a hell of a commute to the regional office, so my bosses let me come in here. That way, they don't have to appoint someone manager of this store—I sort of do double duty."

I smiled and nodded. "Ingenious."

We shook hands, I thanked him again, and then I left. On my way out, I noticed Jimmy hovering on the edge of my vision, watching me nervously. I wondered why he was so edgy. Maybe he thought I was going to become the new director of security at Tech City and he didn't want to be ordered around by a woman.

I smiled and gave him a thumbs-up. Jimmy gave me a dark look, spun on his heel and rushed into Balczeck's office. I stayed around long enough to hear his raised voice. Everyone else in the store seemed to hear it, too, and stopped what they were doing to listen. The words "private eye" and "credit scam" were used before Balczeck finally shut the door.

I left the store with more than Balczeck had given me during our appointment. Now I wanted to know who Jimmy was and where he fit into everything.

FIVE

I WENT HOME intending to settle in for a quiet night with a book and the latest Sheryl Crow CD. But around six-thirty, I bolted upright from my comfortable horizontal position on the sofa. I just remembered the blind date Ma had so coyly set up. Sighing heavily, I cleaned up as best I could. I didn't bother to change, but I added my black fringed-leather jacket. I wanted the guy to know I wasn't all that interested. I tried to remember his name and finally it came to me—Reginald. Reggie. Yuck.

I got to the restaurant at seven on the dot. Sablone's makes great veal, but it's not my favorite meat. Something about the fact that it's really baby cows keeps me from eating it too often. The restaurant is dark, which is nice if you're planning something romantic, but I was actually thinking that maybe it would be better to meet Reggie outside the restaurant. We could go across the street to my favorite place, Santarpio's, which has great lamb and fabulous pizza. I don't have an aversion to lamb. I stayed outside for about fifteen minutes, but after the tenth wolf whistle from guys driving by in cars, I decided to go inside Sablone's and wait. It was chilly outside and I was beginning to feel a little like a streetwalker on a bad corner.

The hostess met me with a smile. "Angie, how are you?"

I peered closer. It was Teresa Marchetti. I'd gone to high school with her and she'd married Bob Leone, the insurance guy I worked for on occasion. "Teresa? Good to see you! What are you doing here?"

She shrugged. "With the kids in school and Bob working all the time, I thought I'd take a job. It's only part-time, but—" she gestured around "—it's a nice place to work. Besides, I'm related." Of course. It's the motto of East Boston: if you need a job, go to your relatives and see who's hiring. Nepotism rules here, but it isn't necessarily bad. If you need a paying job, you can count on your more successful relatives for work. And if you're a successful business owner, hiring your relatives makes sense, especially if you promise them that they'll own half or all of the business someday.

I took a closer look at Teresa. She had put on some weight, but it looked good on her. She was Rubenesque, but with her classically beautiful face and her hair swept up and pinned, she was stunning. She'd never had good taste in clothes back in high school, and the simple ecru tunic over a straight skirt told me that her taste had improved with age.

Although I'd seen Bob many times over the past couple of years, I had turned down his numerous invitations to have dinner with the family. I figured Teresa had enough to do with raising the kids, and I hadn't been all that close to her back in high school. Plus, Bob had been my high-school sweetheart until my senior year.

"You here for dinner alone?" Teresa asked, eyeing the air behind me.

"Nah, Ma set me up on this stupid blind date and he's late."

She frowned. "What's his name?"

"Reginald Giordano."

Her face cleared. "Oh, yes. He called about twenty minutes ago to send his regrets. He was on call at the hospital." She gestured to the almost empty restaurant. It was a Tuesday night, and most people were home with their families.

I shrugged. "What the hell." She sat me at a corner table and I squinted at the menu, finally ordering eggplant parmesan, which wasn't exactly the Sablone special, but I'd had it before and it was pretty good. Teresa came over to make small talk, and I got the impression she wanted to relive those high-school days.

"Remember when we were trying out for the cheerleading squad?"

"You must be thinking of someone else," I replied. "I wasn't interested in cheerleading."

Teresa's brow furrowed. "But didn't you come along because one of your friends was trying out?"

My memory suddenly became clearer. "You mean Raina James. Yeah. Her routine was pretty good—till she fell on her butt during that midair split." She asked about Raina and I told her she was still my best friend and worked for the East Boston police precinct.

When I'd had enough eggplant and high-school memories, I paid the bill and left, promising Teresa I'd come over to her house for dinner one evening. Yeah, when hell freezes over. Like the Bruce Springsteen song, all she wanted to talk about was those glory days.

I was still waiting for my glory days. I suppose some people would say that my peak came with my first case as a private investigator, when I took on a job that involved terrorism. But I take one day at a time, and I'd already put that case behind me. There'd been some newspaper coverage and I'd gotten my name in the paper a couple of times, but Geraldo and Sally Jesse weren't exactly knocking down my door for an interview.

Just before I left Sablone's, Teresa's eyes lit up. "Say, weren't you involved in that case of the retired policeman who was killed? Something about a bomb and the IRA, right?"

I shrugged. "Yeah, that was a couple of years ago, and the publicity netted me a few clients, allowing me to work for myself."

"Wow." Her eyes grew big. "Don't you ever talk about it?"

I smiled. "Not really. Only to my therapist." With that line, I left the restaurant.

WHEN I GOT HOME, the message light was blinking on the answering machine. I played back the tape.

"Hi, this is for Angela." The caller's voice was deep and melodious. "My name is Reginald and we were supposed to meet for dinner tonight. I apologize for standing you up. I'm on call and there was an emergency at the hospital. Can I make it up to you? How about Friday? I have the night off. Give me a call and let me know when and where." He left his number and hung up. I liked his voice. Maybe it wouldn't be so bad to meet him.

I'd been rather relieved, if a little irritated, by the fact that he'd stood me up. But he was a doctor, and was on call, so...I'd give the boy another chance. I called the number he left, hoping maybe he'd answer, but I got his answering machine. I told him Friday would be fine and to meet me at the south end of the food court in Faneuil Hall. I'd be the one wearing a black fringed jacket.

When I hung up, I was feeling more optimistic about the idea of going on a blind date. His voice had sounded all right. I just wondered if he looked like a troll or like Adam Arkin from that TV medical drama. I'd settle for anything in between.

Just as I was ready to turn in early, I heard footsteps on my stairs. A familiar-sounding knock at the door urged me to open it. Wearing the white blouse and black slacks required of the art museum tour guides, Rosa still looked like the fresh-faced college student that she was.

"Hiya, Sarge," she chirped. "Haven't seen you in a while."

She walked past me, her starving-student radar

directing her toward the kitchen. By the time I had followed her in, she was rooting around in my refrigerator for a wine cooler, something that I always kept in supply. Once she'd opened a bottle and taken a sip from a mango-kiwi cooler, she went back to work, pulling out the remainders of an American chop suey that I'd thrown together the other day—elbow macaroni, canned tomatoes, and ground beef. I'd added Romano as a topping. She stuck the plastic bowl in the microwave and punched in three minutes.

"So, you came here to talk or to eat?" I asked.

"Both," she said, offering me a wine cooler. I opted for pouring a glass of chilled red table wine. Plopping herself down at the table, she eyed me over her bottle and asked, "So how was your date?" Then she looked away.

I would have thrown up my hands in disgust, but I still had the glass of red wine in one hand, so I just made a face. "What is this, a family conspiracy? Everyone get together and pick on poor, dateless little Angie." I tried to cross my arms in self-pity, then realized I might spill the wine on my Benetton, so I uncrossed them again and took a sip.

Rosa rolled her eyes at me. "Angie, I was just asking. Ma called me this afternoon, all excited that she'd tricked you into going on this date."

I told her what happened. She giggled.

"What're you gonna tell Ma?"

"I don't know. Maybe I can avoid talking to her for a few days." I love Ma and really miss her if I don't hear from her every day or two, but whenever she gets me into an uncomfortable situation like this, I don't like to tell her the result, even when it hasn't been my screw-up. She always sounds so disappointed and I always end up feeling that it was my fault.

The chop suey was ready and Rosa dug in. I was starting to get hungry just smelling it from across the table. "You wouldn't want to share that, would you?" When she looked up at me, it was as if I'd asked a hungry wolf to share its kill with me. Then she grinned, I got an empty bowl, and she gave me some.

"So, what's school like this term?"

She stopped chewing and swallowed. "I really like it. It's challenging, but I feel as if I get it this time. I'm not being left behind. With all my other majors, I always felt as if I was missing something important. In art history, I seem to be in my element. We're studying twentieth-century artists right now, and I'm trying to decide whether to do my term paper on Winslow Homer, Grant Wood, or Edward Hopper." She thought about it for a moment. "Of course, there's already a little suck-up in the class who'll probably do his paper on Homer."

"Didn't Wood paint 'American Gothic'?" I asked. Rosa looked at me in surprise. "Hey, I'm no chimp! I think you can almost bet that someone will do a paper on him. That's a pretty standard piece." I've always liked Hopper's work the best. He really had a nice feel for the seedy side of life.

"I guess Hopper isn't quite as standard, and there are some nice examples in the museum." Rosa drifted off, her eyes getting a faraway look. I finished off my chop suey and when she was done, she said good night and left. After channel surfing for about an hour, I went to bed early.

WHEN I GOT TO the office the next morning, there were two messages from the temporary agencies that Cynthia's office used, each telling me to come in at eleven o'clock. Since they were down the street from each other, I called one back and set one appointment up for eleven-thirty.

The bulk of the morning was spent on the phone, calling clients who hadn't paid their bill in full and fielding phone calls from prospective clients. I had a call from one place that wanted me to do a repo that evening. I don't think there's a private investigator in the country who enjoys that kind of work—it's definitely under the category of scut work. I locked up the office at ten and took a coffee break before my first meeting at ProTemps.

I entered the place at eleven. The white interior and comfortable office furniture spoke in hushed tones of an outfit that was ready to franchise. The receptionist, who had been efficiently keying in a document, looked up from her computer and gave me a professional smile. You know the kind of smile I'm talking about—the one without an ounce of warmth or spontaneity in it. "How can I help you?"

I explained why I was there. A small frown replaced the helpful smile as she dialed the extension of Margaret Symmonds, the woman I had an appointment with. Speaking low into the phone, she listened carefully, then nodded into the receiver and hung up. Finally, she looked up at me. "She'll be right with you." Then she went back to her typing.

Ten minutes later, Margaret Symmonds materialized from a hallway to the right of the receptionist's desk. She was a tall, well-kept woman in a matching cerise jacket and straight skirt. "Ms. Matelli? I spoke with Ms. Brandywine. She said you were discreet."

I had no idea why discreet was important in this case. I had no plans to go broadcasting the photo of the false Cynthia MacDonald, unless putting her image in front of millions might give me a lead. But I wasn't that desperate yet.

Ms. Symmonds led me back to her office, which turned out to be one of those bright, impersonal places. No pictures of the kids, husband, or pets, no dried roses from a birthday last month, no chocolates on the desk from some past office party. I'd bet my professional reputation that working for ProTemps wasn't much fun. When we were sitting in our respective places—Ms. Symmonds behind her desk and me on a beige, armless office chair, she took control. "Ms. Brandywine is a very big client of ours, so while I wouldn't normally do this—"

She didn't need to say more. I whipped out the photo of the woman. "Has she ever worked for you?"

Ms. Symmonds donned a pair of reading glasses and held the picture away from her as if it were contaminated. Then she took off her glasses, held the photo out to me and said, "No. She's never worked here."

As I took the photo, I stared directly at her, not saying anything. It can make someone nervous and they'll reveal something they might not want to, just to fill the silence. Sometimes it works. Sometimes it doesn't. In this case, it didn't. Or she had nothing more to reveal. She stood up, making it clear that our business was concluded as far as she was concerned.

"Have a nice day," she said. No curiosity in her voice at all. I could have been selling pencils, for all she cared. She didn't know what Amy Brandywine had wanted the ID for, and she didn't want to know. End of story. I thanked her and left.

Fifteen minutes later, I was at the second temp place on Water Street. Temps R Us was a goofy name, and true to form, the office was a series of dumpy, dim little rooms, all done in old varnished wood and pebbled glass, furnished with aged oak desks. The woman in the front office looked weary—she'd seen it all and done it all, and she was ready to retire. Smoke hung thick in the air. This was not a place the Board of Health would approve of as the perfect work environment.

She was collating papers. "Thank God someone came in." She pronounced the word god like *gawd*. "I was about going crazy doing this drudge work."

When she stood up behind her desk, I could see she was short and plump. Her hennaed hair was in an out-of-date modified beehive, and she had on heavy, black-framed glasses. She gave me a motherly smile. "I'm Elsie Douglas. You look like you can type about a hundred words a minute. Am I right?" I type a modest fifty-five words per minutes, but I liked her instantly.

I introduced myself. Throwing her hands up, Elsie smiled, showing a pleasant gap between her teeth. "Oh, yes! A private investigator." She came in close to me and said in a conspiratorial tone, "You're probably on a very sensitive case, but you can tell me. I won't tell a soul."

From another room, I heard a voice boom out, "Don't believe her. She's the worst gossip since Hedda Gabler."

Elsie shouted back, "That's Hedy Hopper, dearie. Hedda Gabler was some character in a play." She turned and smiled at me again. "That's Selma. She co-owns the agency with me." I didn't bother to tell her that it was really Hedda Hopper. She probably knew that and didn't care.

I showed her the photo.

Elsie grunted as she studied it, but she didn't make any comment.

"Selma," she called out. "C'mere a moment."

Selma shuffled in from another room, a cigarette dangling between her lips. I could see in the room behind her a prehistoric computer monitor glowing amber, probably made before the 286s went into production. Selma was squinting, either from the smoke drifting in her eyes or from the old computer, I wasn't sure.

"That damn computer!" Selma glared at the monitor in the next room and made a gesture as if she were slapping an invisible person upside the head. "We gotta spring for a newer model soon, Elsie. I can't work on the damn thing anymore. I'm gonna go blind." She seemed to notice me for the first time—Elsie probably talked to herself most of the time and Selma was used to it.

Elsie introduced us. Selma looked a little disappointed that I was not a client or a prospective temp, but she brightened up at Amy Brandywine's name. "Yes, nice girl. If we could just fix her up with a nice Jewish doctor or something."

"Hey," Elsie interrupted. "What are we, yentas or employment agents?"

Selma ground out her cigarette and eyed Elsie. "I was hoping you'd tell me."

"Oh yeah, Miss Smartypants? How about you take a look at this photo and tell me who this is." Elsie held out the photo.

Selma studied it in the dim light of the office. "This? That's Lisa Browning. Don't you remember her? You tried to pair her off with that no-good son of yours."

"Artie's just having a few financial problems, but he's been getting on his feet lately," Elsie replied in an implacable manner. She turned back to the photocopy. "I remember the face, but you remember the name," she stated matter-of- factly. "We've always worked that way."

I'd been watching the exchange with fascination, and since they were both looking at me, I realized that I was now involved in the decision-making process. "Ah," I said, "but which of you keeps track of the addresses?"

They looked at each other.

Sometimes dumb luck seems to follow me around. The problem was that I didn't know how dumb my luck was. After a flurry of activity that resulted in file drawers being upended and piles of paper being riffled through, Selma emerged triumphant with an address.

I looked at it. "Are you sure it's a good address, not a phony one?"

Elsie answered. "Oh, yes. That's where we send the checks. She never came into the office if she could help it." She shot a look at Selma. "I think she has a kid or something."

They looked at me for confirmation. I smiled noncommittally and thanked them for their help.

"Now, if you ever need work, if the investigation business is a little slow," Selma said, "you come around to us. We'll fix you up with a nice filing job, or if you work with computers, all the better."

They gave me their card—actually, both of them handed me a card at the same time. Then they glanced at each other as if I were the only bait in the sea, so I took a card from both of them and left.

SIX

THE ADDRESS for Lisa Browning was in South Boston. I got my Bronco out of the garage and drove over there. Public transportation in that part of town was a little lean.

The temptation for outsiders is to call South Boston the South End, but those of us in Boston know better. There is actually a separate section of Boston called the South End. It's a lovely place, with garden-filled courts lined with brownstones, and now primarily a gay area. The Boston Ballet makes its home here, as well as plenty of little high-end art and jewelry shops.

South Boston, or Southie, is similar in some ways to East Boston—the town borders a harbor, Old Harbor, and is made up of upper-working-class stiffs. Gentrification has been slowly taking over South Boston for the last ten years. The three-story walk-ups remind me of East Boston, but most of them have been fixed up.

East Boston was still in the throes of gentrification. On the same block, you'd see three buildings that had been renovated to the point that you could imagine living there; then there would be a building with discount siding on it, put up by amateurs; then maybe a couple of buildings that were crumbling around the window sashes and had tarpaper tacked on as siding.

There were plenty of East Boston residents who were resisting the creeping yuppie-ism. Southie residents seemed to have made their peace with the idea. Southie had something else in common with Eastie—the longtime residents were clannish. They didn't like outsiders coming in and changing things. The only difference with South Boston was that the majority of Southie residents were Irish, not Italian.

I drove by Old Harbor by way of Day Boulevard and passed the bathhouse. I'd heard rumors that it was still open, but it looked pretty closed to me. Still, the building was in fairly good shape on the outside. I hoped they didn't tear it down. I could picture the bathers from the Thirties or Forties going in there for a massage or to shower off the sand from the beach. There was something about the look of the building that I'd always liked. Maybe someone would come along and turn it into a restaurant or a small mall.

I turned down Ticknor and looked around for a parking space. Unlike East Boston, parking was hard to come by in Southie. Cars were crammed together in spaces that defied getting in or out. But somehow, people managed to park in spaces that looked smaller than their cars.

I finally found the house—a three-story walk-up off Ticknor, surrounded by a chain-link fence. There were two mailboxes by the door, and one of them was in Browning's name. I rang the bell next to it and waited for a response. No one responded. It was only two o'clock, and I figured that maybe she worked a regular job. Elsie and Selma hadn't mentioned that she was on a job, but temps often register with more than one agency.

I went around the corner and waited in a small retro diner done up in chrome, red, black, and white. I ordered a cup of coffee, then realized that I hadn't eaten lunch, so I ordered a cheeseburger and fries to go.

While I was waiting for my order, anxious to get back to my stakeout across the street from Lisa Browning's apartment, I realized that I was letting a golden opportunity slip by—here I was, in her neighborhood, and I wasn't taking advantage of it to find out as much as I could about her. I tried the waiter first, showing him her photo. He frowned at it while balancing a tray of dirty dishes. "Looks familiar," he said, "but I can't place her. Probably a customer here sometimes, but I don't know her personally." He started to walk away, then said, "I've lived in this neighborhood all my life. Some of the new people who've moved in here, it's hard to keep track of them."

I was contemplating my next move, when I felt a tap on my shoulder. I turned to face an elderly gentleman, the kind of older man who takes a lot of walks and maintains a healthy lifestyle. "Excuse me, but I couldn't help overhearing. Maybe I can be of some help."

I smiled and offered him the photo. "It looks a

little like her, my neighbor, that is. But her name is Lisa Browning, not Cynthia MacDonald." He studied the picture, then looked at me with a grin on his face. "Twins separated at birth?"

"Something like that," I replied grimly. "I take it she hasn't been here long."

"Less than a year," he agreed, "but if you've lived here less than twenty-five years, you're still an outsider." He grinned again. "Ben Twomey's the name."

I shook his extended hand and told him my name.

"So what's she done to deserve this attention? She running a counterfeiting operation in her basement?" His eyes lit up with possibilities. "Maybe she's the madam of a brothel or makes her living hosting all-night poker games."

I shook my head.

He raised his eyebrows, clearly enjoying this guessing game. "Numbers runner?" I smiled. "Hooker? No, I already sort of mentioned that one." He snapped his fingers. "I got it—foreign agent." When I maintained my silence, he furrowed his brow. "Smuggler?"

I shrugged.

Scowling, he tried again. "Not a drug dealer. Please don't tell me she runs a crack house."

I chuckled. "I think you'd know if she were running a crack house."

He thought about it. "Well, there are people coming to her house on a regular basis, but she's usually pretty quiet at night. I've read that drug dealers have people coming and going at all hours, and the police are there just about every night. Nothing like that at this woman's place.''

I shook my head. ''I'm not sure she's done anything,'' I replied. ''I've just been asked to track her down. Once I make sure with my own two eyes that this is the same woman as in the photograph, I turn the information over to my client.''

Ben Twomey leaned in and said in a low voice, ''You must be a private dick.''

I feigned shock. ''How did you ever figure it out?''

He shrugged modestly. ''I spent my working years as a barber. A guy learns to read people that way.''

I was amused, and I was pretty sure he was putting me on as much as I was playing along. The twinkle in his eye was a giveaway. But I didn't mind.

''Seriously,'' I said, ''you've been a big help.''

''Hope you put away the bad guys, whoever they are.'' He left a couple of quarters on his table, got up and patted my shoulder on the way out. ''She usually comes home around this time, and doesn't stay for long. She's gone by five o'clock. I don't know where she goes.''

I put Ben Twomey's name on my list of characters, which includes the old Irishmen down at the Wild Irish Rose Pub, buddies of Uncle ''No-Legs'' Charlie, and my first client, the late Tom Grady. I still occasionally go down to the Wild Irish Rose

Pub on Washington to get together with Bernie, Bertie, and Paddy. They tell such tall tales, it keeps me entertained for hours, and I use those stories to my benefit on occasion when I play poker with Lee Randolph and some of our cronies.

The waiter came back with a Styrofoam box and a bill. After I paid, I made my way out of the tiny diner and down the street to Lisa Browning's brownstone. I sat on a bench across the street, watching for her.

A few minutes after I finished my lunch and I was close to dozing in the sun, a young woman, weighted down with packages and with a little girl by her side, walked up the steps of the house. I perked right up, rubbed my stiff neck, got off the bench and stretched. I didn't make it across the street in time to catch them before the door closed.

I rang the bell and this time, I got an answering buzz. There was no intercom for me to identify myself.

Her apartment was on the third floor. Apparently whoever lived on the first floor also had the second floor. Lisa Browning's door opened on a set of stairs that seemed to go on forever. Near the top, I saw the girl peeking out from behind a banister.

"You're not Daddy," she said. She revealed herself, a solemn-faced, wide-eyed beauty of about four or five. She had golden-brown hair, and her glasses made her look like a little adult. Her lashes were long and lovely, framing warm brown eyes. She was definitely a heartbreaker even at her age.

"Is that your louse of a dad, Jessica?" called a loud female voice. It was followed by a woman who strongly resembled the Lisa Browning in the photo, only a softer version. She must have had a long day because she looked exhausted.

When she saw me, she glared at me as if it were my fault that Jessica's louse of a dad hadn't made an appearance. When she spoke, I understood why she was glaring at me. "You the new girlfriend, honey? I've already told Tim that he's not supposed to send over the lay-of-the-month to pick up his kid. I don't let my kid go with any strange women."

I smiled. No point in antagonizing her before she knew why I was there. "Nope. Wrong woman. Are you Lisa Browning?"

She nodded cautiously, probably not sure what to think of someone who wasn't her ex or her ex's girlfriend. "You're not a process server, are you? Because if that snake is trying to take my child away from me, I'll—"

"I'm sure you would, if I were a process server," I interrupted smoothly. I didn't mention that I served papers occasionally for lawyers. That might not win me many points.

I looked pointedly at the four-year-old hugging her knees, and Lisa seemed to get the picture. "Jessica, honey, I think the Care Bears cartoons are on."

Jessica's eyes lit up. "Oh!" She paused and looked back at me. "You want to come watch with me?"

I wanted to, I really wanted to, but I had an unpleasant task ahead of me. At least I'd won some points with Jessica. I managed a smile. "Thanks for the invite, Jessica, but your mom and I have a little business to discuss."

Jessica nodded as if she was used to being told no quite often. A moment later, the blare of the Care Bears theme song could be heard. Lisa Browning's arms were crossed. "I'd invite you in but—" she nodded toward the apartment—"my place isn't very big, and since you're probably selling something—"

I pulled out the photocopy and handed it to her. "I obtained this from Sam's Car Lease and Rental in Wrentham."

Her face went pale. "This has to be some mistake," she stammered. She wasn't a convincing liar. "It's just someone who looks like me." She handed the paper back to me as if it were about to explode.

I handed her my card. She studied it, then looked at me. "You're on the wrong track. I haven't done anything."

"You rented that car from Sam's, and you drove up to Methuen to Technology Bytes and bought a bunch of stuff. Do I need to call the store and have them read the model and serial numbers of the items you bought, then compare them to the TV and VCR you have in there?" Now I wished I'd pushed the issue to go into her apartment. I wanted to see if there was any stolen merchandise stored there. Maybe I could bribe Jessica to tell me if I offered to watch the Care Bears with her.

She was definitely scared, but not willing to back

down. Her arms were crossed defensively and she shifted from foot to foot. "You don't scare me. You're not a policeman. You can't enter my apartment without my permission."

"I can call the cops and wait outside your apartment until they arrive with a warrant. You can try, in the meantime, to haul the stuff down the back stairs, but your neighbors are pretty nosy, and I'd say someone would be a witness."

She was looking off to the side, trying to come up with a way to get out of this. I'd squeezed her into a corner, and now it was time to give her a chance to get out of it with no more than a slap on the wrist. "Look, Ms. Browning—" I deliberately softened the tone of my voice "—my client, the real Cynthia MacDonald, doesn't want to prosecute a hardworking young mother who made one mistake. Do you have a record?"

Lisa Browning couldn't meet my eyes, but she shook her head.

"And she doesn't want to prosecute the pawn. But if you can give me something to work with, some names, maybe we can help you out of this hole you've dug for youself."

Lisa Browning didn't fit my profile of the hardened criminal. She didn't look as hardened as the license photo taken as Cynthia MacDonald. In fact, she looked more and more like a vulnerable, young divorced mother who'd taken a wrong turn. "You rented that car, and you drove up to Technology Bytes in Methuen and bought a television and VCR last week. I have witnesses who remember you. What isn't clear is if you were acting alone or are working with other people.''

She sagged against the wall, then involuntarily glanced in the direction of the TV set where her daughter was seated, giggling merrily at the stupid antics of the insipid Care Bears. I really wanted to be in there right now, chuckling along with Jessica.

''I was told that…well, that no one would ever know. I just wanted to pay a few bills.'' She said this in a whispery voice, almost as if she was justifying her actions to herself. I wondered if she even remembered that I was there. ''My ex is behind on child support and with Jessica's hospital stay and no medical insurance, I got so that almost anything looked good, even something I knew was illegal. When my boyfriend and Spence told me I could make a little extra money, I—'' She stopped, suddenly realizing that I was there and that she might have said too much. She had. I filed the name ''Spence'' away in my memory bank. She flushed and started blinking back tears. ''I guess I didn't think I was doing any harm. I'm sorry. What will happen to me?''

Lisa was just doing what she'd been told—what someone else had told her to do: ''Here's a fake license and a Social Security number. Go use them to get credit, buy up to the limit, and bring the stuff back to me.'' And she probably got paid a couple hundred dollars after every spree, enough to supplement payment on bills for Jessica's care that her worthless ex wasn't helping her with.

I felt like a heel for scaring her, especially when she glanced at her daughter with fear on her face. I didn't get any feeling of deceit on her part. But I should be contacting my client and giving her this information. Already, I'd confronted Cynthia MacDonald's impersonator and my client probably wouldn't be happy about that. But I had needed to confirm her identity.

"Look," I said, "I'll bet there are other people involved, people who are more accountable than you are. You're part of a ring, right? If you go to the police and roll over on them, you might get immunity from prosecution."

She eyed me as if I was out of my mind. "I'm not part of any ring. This was a one-time thing. My boyfriend,"—I noticed that she was careful not to use his name, but I remembered that she had mentioned a Spence earlier—"gave me the ID to get a few things without having to pay for them." Which meant there were other women using my client's identity.

I shrugged. "I have to take this information to my client, who will take it to the police." I didn't want to leave it like that, but I wasn't sure of what else to say. I finally settled for giving her some advice. "If I were you, I'd make sure my daughter had someplace to stay, and I'd find a lawyer."

She started to bite a fingernail and avoided my eyes. "I don't think I can do that."

"Look, I know this is scary, but you've done something that will get you prison time. I don't think you have a choice right now." She looked up briefly and I looked her in the eyes. "Running isn't an option here, you know. With a child, it'll be easy to trace you. I shouldn't even be talking to you, but I have a feeling that you're a decent human being in a bad situation. If you give yourself up, or at the very least, cooperate when the police come around here, you could get immunity from prosecution. There are others involved, aren't there?"

Lisa lowered her eyes again and started picking at her clothes. "Even if there were a ring, I don't think that would be a very good idea."

"Is it a good idea for you to go to jail and leave Jessica in her father's care? If her father is the vindictive sort, you might not get a chance to see Jessica again, let alone get custody of her again."

An intake of breath told me I'd hit a sore spot with Lisa. "It wouldn't be Tim, it would be his mother. She hates me and thinks I'm a bad mother."

Well, I wanted to say, "You certainly have made some poor decisions." Instead, I said, "You could start to make things right again by going to the police with what you know about the people you work for."

She looked doubtful. "I don't think my boyfriend or his boss would like that." She finally looked up at me. "You must think I'm a horrible person, but I just couldn't make it on my temp salary, and Tim hasn't been paying his child support lately. I'm using the extra money for night classes. I thought that if I took classes in hotel management, I could find a better job." She looked over at her daughter, who was mesmerized by colorful, sickeningly cute animated bears on the television. I noted that it was a new, well-known, name-brand, nineteen-inch television. "I know it's wrong, but everything I've done has been for her."

"I'm sure Jessica would be happy to hear that her mommy stole IDs and credit from innocent people, all in her own name." I couldn't keep the sarcasm out of my voice. Sure, she was a mom, and it's hard to raise a child on your own, but that didn't give her the right to mess up other people's lives. I could almost see Lisa confessing to Jessica years later. What would Jessica's response be? "By the way," I said, "I noticed that you have a brand-new TV in there—get that from your little shopping spree?"

Lisa blanched, but didn't say anything. I guessed she was already practicing remaining silent until she was in the presence of her attorney.

I was finished with her. It was clear that she couldn't up and leave without a trail. She had her daughter, and she had something of a life. But the terrified look on her face when I suggested that she give up her pals told me it was unlikely that she would name anyone.

I softened my voice. "Look, Lisa. You don't owe these people you work with anything but the jail time they deserve. You made a mistake, and now you owe it to your daughter to straighten your life out.''

She avoided my direct gaze and nodded slightly, hesitantly. ''I'll think about it.''

I handed her my card after writing my home number on the back. Then I left.

I DIDN'T HAVE anything planned for that evening, so I made myself a nice salmon fillet for dinner. I baked it in a creamed sherry sauce and heated up some leftover rice and beans. I can't starve myself like some people can. And I pay for it later if I don't exercise.

I decided a little walk would be in order. Things were sure different on the waterfront these days. I'd bought my three-story walk-up a few years ago when my view looked out on the East Boston Harbor. The only thing that separated me from the Boston-proper skyline were some old rotting piers and pilings. An occasional barge or freighter passed by, but it was pretty quiet. These days, I have this incredible waterfront park across the street. Someone in City Hall decided to spruce up the East Boston Harbor. And most residents knew it wasn't because they were due for a community park.

For years, East Boston existed on a drab peninsula in the flight path of nearby Logan Airport. We were an insulated community of lower middle-class, blue-collar Italian families. Today, East Boston is becoming an ethnic mix of Italian, Hispanic, and Asian. I have no problem with the idea of a changing Eastie, but a lot of the older residents grumble about it. Of course, with all of these changes, new crime has been coming into the area. It always does, and it's never directly the fault of the good people who are moving in. But they're blamed all the same.

But getting back to the pretty waterfront park across the street from me—we have one newcomer who keeps to himself—John-John Kennedy has bought himself a nice brownstone up on the hill behind me. Yeah, I'm waiting for him to come over to borrow a cup of sugar any day now.

I suppose if John-John hadn't bought that brownstone, we'd probably still have the eyesore waterfront instead of a park that has raised the value of my place on Marginal Street, but which has also added to the noise element in the neighborhood. I watch parents pushing their kids on the swing set, kids climbing over each other on the nice new tunnel-and-bridge playground set, siblings pushing each other around and screaming at each other. I don't have the nice peaceful view of the harbor that I'd had a few years ago. With John-John living in the neighborhood, I wonder what will happen to our city taxes—will there be an increase, or will the Kennedy machine work hard to keep taxes at the same level?

Along with John-John has come a really undesirable element. A few months ago, an unnamed buyer acquired the Maverick projects. These buildings were built in the waterfront behind Maverick Square station. I knew who bought the projects long before most people did because Ma has so many connections. I mean, why would the Arch-Diocese be interested in buying up property in lower-to middle-income East Boston? Not because of lapsed Catholics like me. No, I was betting that it had more to do with the almighty Kennedy family connection.

The weather was cold and snow was on the horizon. Over and over again, we'd been warned by forecasters that white fluffy stuff was on the way, but I hadn't seen any sign of it. Boston winter weather reminds me of the boor who was invariably invited to a dinner party because of his connections. People always hope the snow will hold off, but are constantly being reminded of its imminent arrival. Sometimes it's late, and sometimes it's early. But it's never on time. Every year, Bostonians prepare for the cold weather long before it ever comes. At the moment, the bad weather was at least a few days off, if not an entire week.

As I walked through the park, I peered across the East Bay. The view of the downtown Boston skyline is clean and neat now that the park is there. Still, I miss the bay the way it used to be—littered with broken pylons and rotting piers, along with the smell of decaying fish. I wonder if the changes in East Boston will have a good effect on us. I suppose there could be some good things to come out of having a Kennedy and the Arch-Diocese in East Boston. Maybe the airplane pattern will be diverted to Chelsea.

After my walk, I went home and tried to read, but

the case kept interfering. I found myself staring into space, thinking about all the pieces of the puzzle. Cynthia MacDonald, whose credit was ruined and who would have to go through legal hell to prove she was a victim; Lisa Browning, who was only trying to keep a roof over her daughter's head and food on the table. I finally put down the book and made some popcorn, with all the butter and salt that isn't good for me, then turned on the television and stared at the screen for an hour. I'm not sure what I watched. When it ended, I looked down at my empty popcorn bowl, thought about making more, but in the end, decided it was time to turn in.

Just before I brushed my teeth, I checked in with my answering machine at the office. Cynthia MacDonald had called, eager to find out how I was progressing on her case. It was too late to return the call. I would get in touch with her in the morning.

When I finally slipped under the covers, at last tired enough to fall asleep, I could think of only one thing—what was I going to report to my client tomorrow morning.

SEVEN

THE NEXT MORNING I decided to go up to Methuen to ask a few questions at Technology Bytes. Although the drive is relatively short—about thirty miles north—I can never count on distance to be an accurate compass of how much time it takes to get to a destination in Massachusetts. Certainly I would have no competition on the drive up—most people commute from the boonies to Boston, and I was going the other way. But there's always road construction and inexplicable tie-ups on a highway like Route 93.

I left at eight, assuming that Technology Bytes would be open by nine. Along the way, I stopped at a convenience store to buy a bottle of water and to call my client. I had sort of hoped I would be able to have lunch up in Methuen or in some small town with a diner, but Cynthia MacDonald insisted on meeting with me during her lunch hour. Which meant I would have to be back to the city by noon.

Methuen isn't hard to get around by car, and Technology Bytes turned out to be right off 93 at the second Methuen exit. It was a burgeoning retail area, and Technology Bytes was sandwiched between an antiques mall and a cellular phone store.

The moment I walked in, a salesman was there to

greet me. "May I help you find something today?" he asked. He was a slender man of about twenty-five who wore wire-rim glasses and a fine blond goatee. MIT grad, or working toward it, I surmised.

"Actually, I'm looking for the manager, Mr. Clemens," I told him, flashing my business card at him. "We spoke on the phone yesterday."

"Private investigator, huh? I remember your call. I've been expecting you." He said this with a faint smile, the kind of confident smile that only an MIT graduate would give.

"Let's go talk in the back," he said. "I'm Chuck Clemens. I own this place."

We sat in comfortable state-of-the-art office chairs. "Coffee?"

I nodded. He got up and went to a small coffee-maker to pour a mug. I smelled it, then sipped it, and was surprised to find that he used a good coffee, probably French Roast.

He noticed my pleased expression. "Methuen's not exactly a hotbed of current culture, but we know how to make a good cup of coffee." He sat. "So tell me again what brings you here? It didn't sound like good news to me."

I briefly outlined what had happened. When I got to the part about the woman who had come in to buy on instant credit, he leaned forward. I took out the photocopy and showed it to him.

He nodded. "She was here a few weeks ago. I remember the rented car. I thought it was strange. You say this isn't Cynthia MacDonald?"

"No. Ms. MacDonald hired me to find this woman. I've actually discovered the identity of the woman, but I needed to have you verify that this photo is of the same woman you sold items to."

"Yes, that's her."

"What did she buy?"

Chuck Clemens got up and walked over to his computer. He hit a few keys and presently a screen came up. "A nineteen-inch television with remote, a VCR, and an answering machine. She seemed interested in a computer, but I got the feeling that she wasn't used to spending money. She told me she would think about it."

I asked if it was a certain brand of TV, and he nodded, then took me back into his small showroom and pointed to the model she had bought. It was the exact model Lisa Browning had in her apartment.

"Can you tell me something?" he asked.

"I'll try."

"Do you think she could be part of some larger scam? You know, we all read in the paper about the rings of people using phony IDs to rip off businesses."

I thought about it. "I don't know. What was your gut feeling about her?"

We walked back to where we'd left our coffee and I took a sip.

"If she was part of a ring," he replied, "she was new at it. She didn't have much self-confidence, and seemed almost apologetic about buying these items. She kept saying, 'I'm getting these things for my daughter and my mother,' as if by telling me that, it wouldn't hurt so much to buy the items.''

I took a few notes and thanked him for his time.

He frowned. "Can you give me her name and address? I'll send her the bill.''

"I'm not at liberty to give you her name right now, but I'll be sure you get it after my client is apprised of the situation.''

He told me he'd take my client's name off the sales receipt, since he wouldn't be able to collect from her anyway. As I was leaving, he said, "I'll think twice before giving anyone else instant credit.''

I GOT BACK to the office with an hour to spare. Rosa and I usually have lunch together on Thursdays, but with my client taking up my lunch hour today, I called the museum where Rosa works on Thursday mornings and canceled our date.

I spent the rest of the hour on the computer, checking out a few backgrounds. Actually, my virtual-reality friend, Skip T, had the pleasure of doing that.

Skip was an anonymous hacker who offered his services to computer-challenged private eyes like myself. He, or she, was able to break through the password system and get information that was no longer being given to the public freely. Okay, it was a bit unsavory, but I, for one, used the information only for my work.

I always e-mailed my requests to him and waited

for his response. I knew him only as Skip T. His handle was an in-joke to those of us who used skip tracers. Skip kept a very low profile. The only way to pay him—or her, I wasn't sure—was through a messenger—always a different one—who came by once a month to pick up the money. Always in cash, no checks or money orders. I once tried to trace him and my search ended in a series of post-office boxes in different states. I finally gave up when I received a message from him via e-mail that read: ''Nice try, Matelli. But I wouldn't be very effective if I was easy to find.''

Since then, I'd made up a number of different scenarios about who Skip really was—it kept me amused when there wasn't any work coming in. One of my backgrounds for him was that he, or she, was a disenchanted member of a Christian cult who was in hiding after damaging testimony against the leader in a court trial. Another story I came up with was that he was an agent in some national security agency who was moonlighting to make a few extra bucks. Either way, we had a good rapport, often sending each other e-mails full of weird quotes from little-known cult movies. He had to be good if I couldn't trace him.

I flipped through my notes and began entering names in my computer. Lisa Browning and Cynthia MacDonald were at the top of my list, but I also included Lisa's ex-husband Tim, and as an after-thought, Jimmy Stiles. I had to call Tech City in Quincy to get his last name, but when I described him, the salesperson who answered knew immediately who I was talking about. I didn't have to think very hard about including Jimmy, the Tech City sales clerk, in my background checks. It wasn't just the weirdly paranoid attitude he took with me in the store, it had a little bit to do with the way he rushed into Balczeck's office and raised his voice about my visit. I just plain didn't like him, and I wanted to see what kind of a weasel he was outside of work.

Skip was in. I had Lisa Browning's Social Security number within a few minutes, and financial statements from her bank within half an hour. Her maiden name was O'Connell; she was twenty-four years old and had attended school in South Boston, graduating with mostly As and Bs. Lisa's first job was working in a bakery. Then she took a job as a filing clerk and doing computer data entry. Skip included a note telling me that it would take longer to get more information about her and the others. I e-mailed back that I looked forward to hearing from him again.

I called Raina, who works as a dispatcher for the East Boston precinct, and asked her to check on Lisa Browning, nee O'Connell. She told me she'd fax over the information when she had a chance to call it up.

While I waited, I had an unexpected visitor. My youngest brother, Albert, stopped by. I always call him Pacino for short because he looks so much like a young Al Pacino. He had recently had his hair cut so it was short in the back with longer hair in the front that fell over his forehead in an appealing manner. A diamond stud winked at me from his left earlobe. That was new. I wondered if it was a real diamond or a cubic zirconium.

"Hey, Pacino, how's it goin'?" I got up, came around the desk and gave him a big hug. "Haven't seen you for ages. What brings you to Boston?"

He grinned. "Business. Thought I'd stop by and see if you want to go to lunch."

Al's business was...well, no one knew. We all knew he had friends who were in the mob, but he never talked about them. Ma was pretty close-mouthed about the subject of what her youngest son did for a living, so we suspected that she knew. But it was generally accepted that Al was in the lower echelons of the Mafia.

Still, he was my brother and I loved him. I just hoped that whatever he did for a living, it wasn't nearly as bad as we all thought.

"Gee, Al, I've got a client coming over during lunch. Any chance you can stick around and maybe have a late lunch?"

"Can do. My meeting was this morning and I'm in town for the rest of the day." Al lives in Providence, Rhode Island, and sometimes drops in to see me when he's in town for business.

"I'll be back in an hour," he said, giving me a salute before fading away.

Raina's fax showed up and I scanned the copy. Lisa Browning's record was clean except for two

parking tickets, each in Quincy around the time of
the car rental. I made a note of it.

Cynthia MacDonald showed up around twelve-
fifteen, about when I'd expected her. It looked as if
she hadn't slept a wink last night. Even with the
makeup job, I detected deep rings around her eyes,
like a raccoon's.

"So what's the verdict?" she asked after she sat
down and put a cigarette between her lips. She
didn't ask if she could light up this time, but I figured I'd given her permission the first time, so what
the hell. I got up and opened a window.

"I got lucky. Your personnel director gave me the
names of the agencies you use, and I showed them
the picture," I began. "She was a temp in your office a few months ago. How do you want to pro-
ceed?"

She frowned. "What's her name?"

I hesitated, wondering what she planned to do
with the information. My client ground out her cigarette in a ceramic paper-clip dish that was on my
desk. I winced as she leaned forward in an intimi-
dating way. "Look, Ms. Matelli, I'm paying you for
information. What I do with it is my goddamned
business."

"I just thought I would offer to go with you when
you make your formal complaint to the police—"

She cut me off. "And I appreciate your efforts.
I'll go to the police alone, but I will have my lawyer
call you to testify. In the meantime, what's her
name?"

I sighed. I was faced with an ethical question here—she had paid for the information, and I should, by all rights, give it to her. But I had a bad feeling about this.

"I guess I'm a little concerned about the way you may use this information. I need assurance—"

She held up a stubby-fingered hand and cut me off again. "—that I won't go over to her house and kill her? How stupid do I look? I'm a successful businesswoman. Why would I jeopardize all of that for some lowlife scumbag who has to rip off other people's identities because she can't get her own credit?"

I reluctantly gave up the photocopies I'd made for her. "Lisa Browning isn't a scumbag. At least her four-year-old daughter probably doesn't think so. I think she's just in way over her head." I said the next thing before I had a chance to think about how it would be received. "I urged her to give up the names of the others in the credit-card scam, but I really don't think she's part of any ring."

My client looked at me as if I was mentally challenged. "You actually talked to her? Are you insane?"

"What do you mean?"

"You told her who you were and why you were there? What kind of private investigator are you anyway?" She was trembling and her face had turned a lovely shade of beet-red. I could understand. It hadn't been the smartest thing I'd ever done. Okay, so it had been downright stupid. I tend to be impulsive. I have to learn to control that behavior. It gets me into trouble a lot.

"Apparently not a very good one," I told her, "from your reaction. Look, she has a four-year-old daughter, and she seemed to be genuinely remorseful. She seemed to realize that she'd been caught, and it seemed to me that she just was desperate to make a little extra money. It didn't occur to her that she was hurting people."

Cynthia had crossed her arms. "And now she's going to up and move in the middle of the night while we're giving our statements to the police. I'll have to start all over again." The unsaid words, "with another private investigator," hung between us, as obvious as neon letters.

I shrugged. "I don't think she's going anywhere. She has a kid."

My client rolled her eyes heavenward and gestured to the ceiling, sort of the way Ma does when she says, "I'm cursed! I'm cursed with children who don't care!"

"I truly don't think she's going anywhere. But if she does disappear, I found her once, I'll find her again," I said. "And I'll do it on my dime, since you feel I've gotten you into a bad situation. But if we move now, we can probably get a report filed before tomorrow, and the police will visit her tomorrow morning."

Before she could respond, Albert popped his head into my office. "You ready to go to lunch yet, Sarge?"

I looked back at my client, who was eyeing Albert. He'd stepped all the way inside at this point and I saw he was carrying a small package. I wondered if it contained a new gun or something equally dangerous. Cynthia turned her attention back to me. "All right, we'll do it your way. You give me the papers and I'll go to the police. I'll contact you about talking to them when I'm finished, all right?"

Reluctantly, I agreed. I gave her copies of my report, including Lisa Browning's address and phone number, and we three left the office together.

Cynthia smiled at Albert. I hadn't thought my client, who resembled one of the gargoyles in the Disney *Hunchback of Notre Dame* movie, had a flirtatious bone in her body. It wasn't a pretty sight, but I knew the effect Albert had on women.

I jumped in, slightly annoyed by her cloying attitude. "This is my brother Albert. Albert, Cynthia. Cynthia is one of my clients."

He shook her hand solemnly. "My sister usually forgets to introduce me to her friends. Nice to meet you."

I refrained from mentioning that Cynthia wasn't a friend, she was a client.

"What do you do, Albert?" she asked. I was pretty sure she wasn't his type. It wasn't just her battleship shape or her plain face—Albert actually likes his women a little zaftig and doesn't mind if they aren't model-pretty. The fact is, Albert doesn't like women who come on too strong, and she was doing everything wrong. I didn't bother to clue her in. Instead, I listened to Albert's response.

"I, uh, I'm in management."

"Oh," she trilled.

I was past the disgusted stage.

Out of what I was positive was politeness on Albert's part, he asked her what she did for a living.

"I'm in financial management. Stocks, bonds, CDs. I work for an investment firm. Do you have a portfolio yet?"

I was surprised by Albert's pensive expression. "Not yet, but I've been thinking about it. Who do you work for?"

She whipped out a business card. "I can set something up for you whenever you want."

He studied the dignified gray card. "Okay, that'd be fine. I'll be in touch."

She walked away, trying to look sultry but just coming off looking like the crotch of her pantyhose was starting to creep down toward her knees. I suppressed a laugh. It's not polite to laugh at clients, especially when they leave your office in a hostile mood.

"Where do you want to go?" Albert asked, bringing me back to the present. I noticed he was tucking my client's card in his breast pocket.

I suggested a little place near the North End on the marina; it wasn't fancy but had fabulous food.

The lunch crowd was looking pretty light, but it was past one o'clock. I ordered pasta with shrimp and scallops in a garlic-wine sauce, and Albert ordered the broiled scrod.

While we ate our Caesar salads, I decided to risk butting into Albert's business. "So why are you in town today?"

Albert was quiet for a moment. "I had to see my lawyer."

Little bells went off in my head. I hoped Albert didn't hear them. All I could think of was *Oh, my God, he's in serious trouble. Ma's not gonna be happy.*

"Oh," was all I could manage to say.

And of course Albert managed to turn the conversation back to me. "So what's this Cynthia's problem?"

"Besides tight pantyhose?" I asked.

He thought about my response for a moment, then laughed. "Oh, yeah. Is she that way with every guy?"

I shrugged. "She's not exactly a close personal friend. And I can't tell you what her business is about. If you make an appointment with her to discuss financial matters, I'm sure she'll tell you all about it while she undresses you with her eyes."

"Please," he replied with a shudder. "I hope there's no sexual harassment when I make an appointment."

I raised my eyebrows in surprise. "You mean to say you're really gonna go there? You know what she wants, and it ain't your bank account."

He grinned at me as the waitress came up to our

table with our respective meals. "Oh, yeah? Wait'll she gets a look at my bank account. She may change her mind."

I ignored his comment. I didn't feel like talking Mafia with him.

Instead, I came straight to the point. "So what's going on, Albert?"

"What do you mean?"

"I mean," I said patiently, "why are you here? Why did you have to see a lawyer?" Scenes from the movie *Wiseguys* danced in my head.

He scowled. "It's nothing illegal. Just some financial stuff." He picked at his scrod. I was tempted to play Ma and tell him to eat his food, but whenever I find myself starting to act like Ma, I try to squelch the impulse.

"Okay, okay, just trying to make small talk." I couldn't stand it anymore. Don't ever call me subtle. I leaned forward. "Albert, spill. We all want to know what you do for a living, and Ma's worried."

"What do you think I do for a living?" he asked in a maddeningly calm way.

"Damn it, you're not normal, Albert."

He raised his eyebrows. "Why do you say that?"

"Because you ask these incredibly annoying questions and your sister wants to kill you." I calmed down. "Besides, I think you like the mystique of everyone thinking you're a button man."

That got a laugh out of Albert. "That's what everyone thinks I do?"

"Come on," I replied. "You know they do. And you love every minute of it."

"Well, rest assured, big sister, that what I do for a living is perfectly legal and is poised to become very profitable soon." He toyed with his fork. "What did you mean about me not being normal?"

"Well, you don't strut around boasting about your job and all the broads you've laid." I gestured at him. "And come on, Albert, if you were my sister instead of my brother, you'd win the beauty contest hands down, even with Sophia in the running." I took a sip of my wine. "And as a woman, let me tell you, bro, if you weren't related to me, I'd be after you in a flash."

He waved his hand. "You're a good-looking woman, Angie. You don't give yourself much credit."

I waved my hand back. "Agh!" We grinned at each other. "So how's that for small talk?"

"Speaking of small talk," Albert said, still smiling wickedly, "I hear that you had a blind date the other night."

I winced, and could see that Albert was taking immense pleasure in my discomfort. And that was aside from the fact that he'd also managed to weasel out of telling me what he did for a living. "He stood me up."

"Oh, really?"

I found myself getting on the defensive on behalf of a guy I hadn't met, and might not ever meet. "Yeah. He's a resident at Mass General. He was called into work. He sounded nice. We agreed to meet on Friday."

"Tomorrow. Where you gonna go?"

I shrugged. "We're meeting at Faneuil Hall. So who're you dating these days?"

Albert had gotten a divorce from Sylvia, whom he'd been married to for six years. It hadn't been unexpected. There weren't any children, and from the way she treated our family, it was good riddance in the Matelli collective opinion. Ever since the divorce was final, Albert has dated a succession of women. I'd heard the complaints from Ma, because she's always hoping the next one will be the permanent replacement. I keep telling her, "Leave Albert alone. When he finds the right one, he'll introduce her to the family."

But the truth is that I'm as concerned as Ma. I just don't interfere as much. Of course I don't have the right to interfere the way Ma does. Albert will take that from his own mother—we all take it from her because we never contradict Ma—but from his older sister? Nah.

Albert stopped in mid chew and thought about it. "The last girl I dated was from my high school."

I gave him a look.

"No, I mean, I met her at my high-school reunion this summer. Her name is Andrea. I had to go back to my yearbook to remind myself of who she was back then. She'd been overweight and frizzy-haired, but boy, has she changed." He reached into his wallet. "I have a picture from when I took her to Disney

World in September." He handed over a photo that showed him with a nice-looking woman, an Amazon. She wasn't overweight, though she did have a curvy figure, and her smile was bright. Her hair was still frizzy, but it was styled now.

I am only three years older than Albert but I didn't recall this woman in school. "Andrea," I mused to myself. "She doesn't look familiar. Some people do change after high school."

"She was in the band. Played trumpet."

I tried to recall her—she just didn't come to mind. I had skipped most of the homecoming events, so that might have something to do with my hazy memory. I didn't want to remind Albert of my laissez-faire attitude back then. He'd been convinced I was a druggie. In fact, I wasn't. I just hung out with a crowd that had the reputation and nothing to back it up.

"So are you still seeing her?"

Albert reached for another roll. "She seems to have cooled our relationship. I'm not sure why."

I could understand. A guy who doesn't tell you what he does for a living can be trouble. But I didn't mention that to Albert. If he ever asks me, I might...

"So, Angie, what could be her trouble?" he asked.

Oooh, boy. I hated to get into this. What could I say to him? "Albert, when she asks you what you do for a living, have you ever told her?"

He was silent for a moment. Then he looked me in the eye. "What do you think I do, Sarge?"

I'd have to give him a straight answer. "I think you're a wiseguy, Albert. But I'm not sure she'll accept that."

I waited for a reaction, but he just chewed on his buttered roll and seemed to be deep in thought. I went back to my meal for a while.

Finally, he said, "You're right, Angie." He took out an American Express card. It was platinum. "I'd better be straight with Andrea if I want to keep her." He patted his mouth with his napkin and signaled the waitress for the bill. "My treat today." We got up and he leaned over to kiss me on the cheek.

"Thanks, bro." I hadn't gotten the information I'd hinted at so broadly. I still didn't know what he did for a living, but at least Andrea might solve the mystery—if she turned out to be his true love.

As we headed out the door, Albert suddenly hit his head with the palm of his hand. "I almost forgot to give you this." He held up the bag he'd been carrying since he came into my office. "Stephanie's birthday is Saturday."

Oy, I'd forgotten. I took the bag and looked inside. It was a doll. Sort of. I pulled it out of the bag. It was something called Itty Bitty Kitty, a cat-faced doll. The package was hot-pink and turquoise, and in bright yellow letters, it said, "Comes with three changes of clothes! Each doll has real whiskers and cat eyes that change color when held up to the light! Collect 'em all!" I swear, if I saw one more exclamation mark, I was gonna get a twitch in one eye.

The doll had an insipid look on its catlike face.

"Real whiskers?" I looked up at him, the skepticism showing. I had this vision of the doll factory where they had cats on conveyor belts and workers with tweezers pulling whiskers out of the cats, one by one. "You're kidding."

With a serious look on his face, he examined the package. "Yeah, that should be changed, shouldn't it? PETA'll think, uh, the company goes around pulling whiskers off of live cats."

I stared at him. He looked at me and grinned. "So you haven't gotten Stephanie anything yet, have you?"

I shook my head. "I'll find something before Sunday." I looked back at the Itty Bitty Kitty doll. "You think she'll fall for this?"

"Yeah. And there's a whole wardrobe of this stuff coming out. I think they'll have a dollhouse as well. Maybe later in the year."

I gave my brother a suspicious look. "How do you know so much about this company?"

He looked stricken, then seemed to recover. "Uh, I bought into it earlier this year. Lots of stock. I have a couple thousand shares. I think this doll'll be bigger than Barbie."

I raised my eyebrows. "I thought you told Cynthia that you don't have a portfolio."

He seemed to think about that longer than he needed to. "Well, I guess I assumed a portfolio was a group of stocks from different companies, not just a lot of stock from one company."

I let that one go by. Albert is smarter than that,

but there must have been a reason why he was evading the question. "Since when did you get interested in dolls and other toys?"

He grinned. "Since I started investing my money in stocks."

We hugged and parted, with Albert promising to see me at Ma's this coming Sunday. I watched my movie-star-handsome brother walk away and the effect he had on women who passed him. It was fun to see women do double takes and lick their lips when Albert walked by.

On my way back to the office, I thought about Albert's admission to buying stock in a new toy company. Maybe that's where his money came from. That platinum AmEx card he'd flashed at the restaurant showed he wasn't doing too bad financially. Maybe I should invest in this new toy company. I made a mental note to ask Albert more about the company that made Itty Bitty Kitty the next time I saw him.

EIGHT

I CHECKED MY e-mail when I got back and saw that
Skip had forwarded loads of information for me to
sort through. Lisa'd had a few parking tickets, and
her ex had been picked up once for assault. Other
than that, his record was clean.

Cynthia, interestingly enough, had a sealed juvenile record that Skip had managed to break into. My
client had been arrested at age sixteen for assaulting
a teacher. That was interesting and something that I
filed away for future reference.

Jimmy Stiles was clean, but his financial statements showed that he had lots of money in the bank,
and his credit report told me he owned, free and
clear, a Mazda Miata. It was unusual but not unusual
enough to dig any deeper. His money and car probably came from a rich aunt who doted on him, and
working at Tech City might suggest that he had a
strong work ethic. I put the reports aside to examine
more closely at a later date.

I thought about it for a few minutes. There wasn't
much I could do in the middle of rush hour. Stores
would be closing, people would be going home to
make dinner, so I locked up my office and went
home.

I had a date to go to an early movie that night

with my friend Raina. When I met up with her, I told her about my case and she thought it sounded horrible.

"We've been getting a lot of those types of cases coming through the station," she said. "And there's very little that can be done. They all sound alike— the wrong person gets some poor schlub's Social Security number and takes it out for a drive, and before the victim knows it, he's paying for someone else's shopping spree."

I knew this, but I also knew that I paid for these crimes with higher prices, higher insurance rates, and less trust on the merchant's part, which translates into higher security costs.

We went to a small art theater in Boston proper, paid for popcorn drowned in fake butter and as we watched the film, I could hear my arteries clogging. *Strictly Ballroom* was an Australian film that I'd heard good things about. It surpassed my expectations. I've always had a fondness for films and books that take a quirky look at some facet of the human condition, especially if they make me laugh and cry at the same time.

It was around eight-thirty when we finally emerged from the theater. Crossing the street to the T station, I was making the point that *Strictly Ballroom* wasn't a movie about ballroom dancing so much as about following your own dreams instead of staying comfortable with the norm. I heard the sound of a car revving its engine somewhere nearby, but intent on finishing my point, it wasn't until I heard tires squealing and saw the deer-in-headlights look on Raina's face that I knew we were in trouble.

I had just enough time to glance at the headlights racing toward us before spinning around, pushing Raina away from the oncoming car and diving toward the curb, using an *ukeme,* a shoulder roll. I could feel the breath of the car as it whizzed past me, slamming into the car in front of me. The driver had swerved toward me as I tried to get away. I could feel the side of the car brush up against the sole of my shoe as I made it to safety.

I ended up slamming my hip on the curb, and one of my legs was tucked up uncomfortably underneath me. I was able to turn my head in time to watch the killer car fishtail its way down Mass Ave. Unfortunately, it was too far away for me to read the license number.

"Man, what was that guy on?" one renegade from the '60s commented as people gathered around us.

"I bet he was on angel dust. I think their eyes glow red. I swear his eyes were glowing red," said a voice from farther back in the crowd.

"Nah, that's stupid. He's probably some mob hit man and missed his target. These two chicks were in the way," theorized a third faceless party.

Other indignant voices of passersby chattered on among themselves about what a close call we'd had with death. Two people who came forward to check on us identified themselves as off-duty doctors, and a nurse happened to be nearby as well. While one of the doctors inspected me for damage, the other checked out Raina. I wanted to respond to the people who thought that a woman couldn't be rubbed out by the mob as easily as a man. But I wasn't in the mood to defend Albert's probable employers, and I was busy having my ankle checked over by the older of the two doctors.

"How does this feel?" my doctor, a distinguished-looking, gray-haired gentleman, asked as he squeezed my ankle.

"Like you're squeezing my ankle. It doesn't hurt. Honestly." I figured I'd probably limp for a day or two, but I was sure I'd be fine. I'd had worse injuries during an enthusiastic aikido class. I'd just ice the ankle, take some ibuprofen, and elevate it for the night.

"You're damn lucky it wasn't your head," said the doctor in a gruff but lovable manner. "It was almost as if that car *wanted* to hit you."

No shit, Sherlock, I thought as I stood up with some help from the woman who identified herself as a nurse. She took a packet of ibuprofen from her purse. "Here, I always carry this with me." I took it and thanked her.

"Rest, ice, compression, and elevation," the doctor said, helping me up and surveying the damage. "Maybe we should call an ambulance. You should get that ankle X-rayed, just to be sure."

I could see the dollar signs adding up. I didn't have health insurance yet because, like most self-employed people, I'd had to cut back on something, and I figured that if I were ever really sick, I'd just have to go on the dole. It wasn't a pleasant thought, but if I was gonna make my mortgage every month and maintain a business that was as easy to predict as the path of a tornado, I had to give up something.

"Thanks, Doc, I'll look into it."

I looked over to see if Raina was all right. She was flirting with the doctor who was checking out her shoulder. He was younger, less stodgy, and good-looking. I was wishing that I'd gotten Raina's doctor, when a plump black woman came up to me with what looked like a squished animal that she was holding by the tail. As she came closer, I realized that it had once been my purse.

"I found this in the middle of the street. Is it yours?"

I took it gingerly. "Thanks," I replied as I examined it.

"I'm sorry, I wish I'd found it in better shape." She genuinely looked as if it were her fault.

"I'm sorry, too," I said and managed to grin. "But it isn't your fault."

Her brow darkened. "I saw what happened from across the street. That car looked as if it was gunning for you."

I had already figured that out, somewhere between when Raina and I started to cross the street and when the driver gunned his engine, but still I went a little cold at her words.

"You didn't happen to get the license plate, did you?"

She shook her head. "No, I'm afraid it happened too fast."

"Do you remember anything about it?"

She looked thoughtful for a moment. "It was a sporty little car. Don't know much about the names of those things."

I thanked her again, took her name and phone number as a witness, and the doctor's number as well, then went over to see how Raina was doing. She was exchanging phone numbers with the doctor. He touched her arm once and when she turned to check on me, I was giving her my "you-are-the-cat-that-ate-the-canary" look. She just gave me a smug grin and tucked the business card into her three-dimensional purse. Then she looked down at my two-dimensional purse. "What happened?"

"One of us didn't come out alive, and I think it was my purse."

She shuddered. "Was that car trying to kill us?"

"You didn't tick off any of the fine, upstanding citizens who come through the doors of the precinct, did you?"

She shook her head. I looked at my watch—it had been close to 45 minutes since we got out of the movie and I was starving. Almost being run over can do that to me.

"Then he must have been after me, kimo sabe," I said. "I'm getting a strong sense of deja vu. I was attacked just like this on my first case, and the next day, my client was found dead" I crossed my arms, suppressing a shudder.

She touched my arm. "Do you want to check on her?"

I thought about my current client, who was still alive, as far as I knew. I didn't like Cynthia Mac-Donald, and although I was sure there were plenty of people who might be gunning for her, I didn't think she was a target in connection with the credit-card scam. Still, it wouldn't hurt to check up on her. She might even be touched enough to give me a bonus, but I doubted that.

"I'm not sure where she lives, but I think I have her home phone number in here." I dug around in my squished purse, which held a mashed wallet—I swore I'd had more money in it, but when I counted, the bills were all there. Maybe they just looked flatter after being run over. I found Cynthia's business card—with her home phone number on it—and a pay phone, and dialed her number. It rang four times before an answering machine picked up.

Her answering-machine message was as brusque as she was: "I'm not here. Leave a message at the tone and I'll get back to you."

"Cynthia, are you there? If so, pick up. This is Angela Matelli. I need to talk to you, make sure you're all right." If she was there, she wasn't picking up. Why would anyone want to kill Cynthia, other than the fact that she wasn't a very nice person? I shook my head and decided I was being paranoid. The car that almost took me out might not have anything to do with my client.

"She didn't answer?" Raina looked anxious. She

didn't even know Cynthia, and there was no reason to think that my client not answering the phone and the driver who tried to kill me were connected. Unless, of course, you'd had an experience similar to mine. Then anything was possible.

We stopped in a convenience store and I managed to pry a Boston phone book out of the sullen clerk behind the register. I looked up Cynthia MacDonald and sure enough, a C. MacDonald was listed with the same phone number I had dialed. I made a note of the address, then decided to call my office answering machine. I try to check it once a night in case any repo work comes my way; repo companies don't always work on a nine-to-five schedule.

I had two messages.

"Angela, I just want to apologize for my behavior today." Cynthia's voice was sullen, as if she didn't want to apologize but her mother had told her it was the proper thing to do. "You're a professional and I'm sure you used good judgment when you confronted the woman…" she paused and I heard paper crackle "…Lisa Browning. I just want you to know that I'm going to the police tomorrow. You said you'd go with me. Please call me first thing in the morning and tell me where and when I should meet you."

Despite my client's reluctant apology—it was clear that admitting she was wrong was hard for her—I felt a certain pressure lift off my shoulders. I resolved to call her back in the morning.

The second message was a surprise. "Ms. Matelli?'' The voice was small and just above a whisper. "This is Lisa Browning. I need to see you. I've decided to do the right thing, but I'm afraid someone knows that I'm planning to go to the police. I don't want to do anything until I hear from you.'' She recited her number and hung up.

Raina was cruising the snack section, picking up a bag of candy here, a bag of cheese balls there. From Lisa's tone, I got the feeling that whatever she wanted to tell me couldn't wait, so I called her right away.

She answered on the first ring. "Hello?''

"Lisa? This is Angela Matelli.''

She was breathless. "Ms. Matelli, I think I'm in trouble. I'm afraid.''

I immediately thought about her daughter. "Is Jessica there with you?''

"No, she's spending the night with her father.''

"Can you tell me about the trouble you're in?'' As if true name fraud wasn't enough, I thought.

"Can you come over? I'll pay you. I don't have much money in the bank, but—''

I glanced over at Raina. She had already started in on the bag of cheese balls.

"I'm with a friend,'' I told her. I thought about almost being killed earlier. "Can you meet me somewhere?''

"I'm afraid to leave my house.''

"I'll be there as soon as I can. In the meantime, call the police,'' I suggested. "Tell them you thought you saw a prowler on the premises. Then go to a neighbor's apartment. I can be there within—" I checked my watch; it was about nine-thirty—"half an hour. Before we hang up, I have to ask you about something that happened to me to-night, Lisa."

I could hear an intake of breath on her end. "What?"

"I was almost run down by a car. Does that have anything to do with who you are afraid of?"

She was silent. I heard a bang in the background. In a small whisper, Lisa said, "I think someone's trying to get into my apartment. The doorknob moved." I heard a thud as if someone was knocking real hard. "Oh, my God—" Then I heard a crash and she let out a yelp. "What are you doing here?" She wasn't talking to me. I heard the phone drop and the sounds of a struggle.

"Lisa," I said loudly. "Who's there? Lisa!" I turned and called to the clerk. "Call the police. Someone's being assaulted." I tried to remember her address, but my mind went blank.

I was aware that customers in the convenience store were turning to look at me.

"Angela?" I could barely hear Lisa. She was sob-bing, and her voice was muffled, as if she were be-ing dragged away from the phone. "Don't hurt me. P-please don't hurt me."

"Lisa?" I yelled again. "Goddamnit, you pervert. Leave her alone."

"Help! Angela! Call nine-one-one. Call the—" The phone went dead.

I got through to a dispatcher. "I was just on the phone with a friend when someone broke into her apartment. She is in physical danger." My mind was focused and I gave Lisa's address, hung up, and turned to Raina. "Do you mind if we—"

Raina nodded, way ahead of me. The clerk hadn't moved since I last yelled to him to call the police. I turned to him and said, "Thank you so much for your help. I hope you're as quick with the phone when you're being robbed." He just nodded slowly, transfixed by the drama that had happened in his store. There's a reason some people are working at a convenience store. We got out of there and headed for the street.

"You don't have to go with me," I told Raina.

She shrugged. "I'll be your alibi. Knowing your luck, the police will think you broke into her place."

I shuddered at the thought. Raina talked as if Lisa were already dead. The funny thing was that I got the same feeling. The police wouldn't get there in time.

I hailed a passing cab and we got to Lisa's place in Southie in under half an hour. I started to think about getting there and finding that the police hadn't gotten there yet. What would I do? Would the killer still be there, lurking about to see if I showed up? Was I putting Raina in peril, too?

The street was already blocked off by several police cars, their lights flashing, drenching the area in a red glow. A few neighbors had come out of their houses to see what was happening. The cab let us off across the street and we walked over to the nearest policeman.

"Is she all right?" I asked.

He was a skinny kid, fresh out of the academy. His eyes bulged for a moment, then he looked official. "Is who all right, ma'am?" he asked. "Do you know something about this situation?"

Lisa Browning was nothing more than a "situation" now.

"Lisa Browning. She was on the phone with me when it happened," I explained. "I was the one who called it in. Is she all right? Did you get here on time?"

The officer hesitated, too green at his job to know what to do. "I'm afraid I can't give you that information," he finally replied, "but I'm sure Detective Sturgeon can make that decision."

The officer let Raina and me through, then ordered me to stand on the perimeter of the crime scene while he got the detective to come talk to me. It was about ten minutes before someone came out.

I didn't need the young patrolman or Detective Sturgeon to tell me one thing: the body bag made it official—Lisa Browning was dead.

off across the street and he walked to within ear—
an policeman.

as she all right? I asked.

His . . . turned me b remained then it shifted to
friend. Is she all right? She was

NINE

DETECTIVE RANDALL STURGEON was in his mid-to
late fifties and looked as if he'd seen it all. He had
the kind of face that made you think of Elvis's song
"Hound Dog." He took my statement. I explained
where I was when the victim was killed.

"You were on the phone with her when she was
attacked?"

"I heard him enter her apartment with force," I
said. "I think the intruder intended to kill her all
along and—"

Sturgeon interrupted me. "It could have been a
home invasion."

I shook my head. "No, she specifically suggested
that she knew the intruder." I had a thought. "Is
anything missing?"

"We haven't taken an inventory yet."

I explained why I was interested. His eyebrows
rose when I got to the part about the television, the
VCR, and the answering machine. He scribbled
notes on his pad of paper. "Looking over the crime
scene, I noted that there wasn't a television or VCR
in the apartment. It looks like it may be a home
invasion, or possibly some of her associates turned
against her."

I needed to talk to my client before releasing information about Lisa Browning's connection to the credit-card-scam ring. I turned the subject back to the present. "How did she die?"

"Blunt instrument. Very messy. She didn't die quickly." Sturgeon sounded angry and disgusted. I didn't blame him. He signaled the end of the interview by asking for verification of my name, phone, and address.

I took out a business card and handed it to him. "Here. You might need my work number as well."

His pen jabbed the air, pointing to Raina. "Who's this?"

"Raina James," my friend said, spelling her last name with exaggerated care.

He looked up, his face giving nothing away. "You a comedienne or something?"

"I work for the East Boston precinct as a dispatcher," Raina replied, crossing her arms. "I'm Ms. Matelli's alibi."

He waved a hand in the air. "She doesn't need an alibi. Several officers saw the cab pull up down the street and let you two girls out."

I could see Raina bristle at the detective's reference to us as "girls." I had enough trouble getting him to take me seriously, I didn't need Raina lecturing him on the fine points of feminism.

"Uh, Raina, I need to ask the detective some questions in private, so could you wait for me over there somewhere?"

Raina shot me a hurt look, spun on her heel, and marched over to a patrol car. A moment later, she was flirting with a young, hunky patrol officer. By the time I got done, she'd have forgotten all about her abrupt dismissal.

When the detective was finished writing up his comments, he looked at me appraisingly, sighed, and closed his notebook.

"You have no official standing here, Miss Matelli. But I appreciate your cooperation and I am aware that you may have information that is pertinent to this investigation. Can you come to my office early tomorrow morning to finish our interview? We normally take witnesses in and get their statements when we arrive on a scene, but you weren't technically on the scene during the murder, so I can give you that much leeway."

"Thank you, Detective."

He held up his finger to show that he wasn't finished. "But I would like you to bring in the information that you've gathered in this case you're working on that involved the victim."

"I'm sorry," I replied, "but if you want me to give up the name of my client, I can't do that. Not unless I have direct knowledge that my client is involved in this homicide."

Sturgeon frowned. "It would be easier if I could clear this up—"

"I understand what you want—you don't want me withholding information that may lead to the arrest of the suspect or suspects." I waited for him to nod, then I went on. "And I will cooperate with you, but I cannot divulge the identity of my client." I was treading a fine line right now, skirting the law but remaining loyal to Cynthia MacDonald. But the truth is that I wasn't so sure she *hadn't* killed Lisa Browning.

Sturgeon looked as if he was on the verge of giving orders to have me escorted to his precinct and held there indefinitely.

"Look, Detective, I've worked with the police before, and I can give you the names of several detectives in other precincts who have worked with me on cases," I said. "I can promise you that I won't withhold vital information from you."

He looked grim, not too happy with me, but none of us looked too happy about being up at this hour with a dead woman in an apartment in South Boston. I got the feeling that he saw the private eye as sleazy, similar to a lowlife lawyer—if that isn't an oxymoron in itself. We were a necessity, but one he didn't have to like.

I went over the facts one more time, leaving out my client's name. Detective Sturgeon nodded and asked a few more questions to pinpoint what seemed like minutiae, but I knew very well from my work in the Criminal Investigation Division of the Marines that the smallest detail can be what brings a killer to justice.

"I'd like you to be at my precinct tomorrow morning at eight."

I resisted the urge to salute. I nodded and left.

"You ready to go home?" Raina asked. She'd been waiting in the back of one of the patrol cars.

It seemed that only now I noticed the details of the crime scene—the red lights flickering in the black night, the radio's static that was often broken by the sound of dispatchers repeating crime-in-progress information in a cryptic monotone that only a cop could decipher after years of experience. The body had already been loaded into the ambulance and the officers were beginning to wind up the crime scene.

The lab crew had packed up and left a few minutes ago, and the neighbors were beginning to thin out; the excitement winding down meant it was time to retire to bed to try to get a decent night's sleep so they could gossip at the water cooler tomorrow. I caught sight of Ben Twomey. He was one of the few bystanders who wasn't dressed in pajamas and a robe. He looked as if he had just come home from a night out at a pub. He caught me staring at him, smiled faintly and nodded in my direction. I smiled and nodded back. I made a note to call him tomorrow.

Raina shook my arm. "Angie? Did you hear me?"

I blinked, back in the real world again, a world where a young mother, desperate to make a good life for her daughter, had just been murdered. "I'm ready to go. I was ready back when that car almost killed us." We fell silent as we trudged away from the crime scene toward one of the major streets. I could see that Raina was worried, but I had other things on my mind.

I'd been thinking about my client and the possibility that she may have killed Lisa Browning in a fit of rage. Sure, she'd assured me that she had no intention of harming the woman who had ruined her credit, but it wasn't as if I couldn't imagine my client wielding a baseball bat, standing over Lisa's body. It was all too possible, especially after learning Cynthia had been arrested for assault as a juvenile. I needed to reassure myself that Cynthia was snug in her bed, wrapped in a blanket—not wandering the streets with blood on her hands.

"I can't go home yet, Raina," I said. "I have to go check on my client, see if she's home and all right." The more I thought about it, the more certain I was that Cynthia hadn't killed Lisa Browning. Surely she'd know she'd be the first suspect. It wasn't like I was a priest—confidentiality in my profession didn't cover aiding and abetting a murderer. I may not like Cynthia, but I didn't think she was a killer. "You might as well go home," I added.

"I might as well go along. Probably nothing will have happened. Your client's probably out with friends," was Raina's reply. What loyalty. Still, I had a hard time imagining Cynthia MacDonald as having any friends. Then Raina added, "Besides, if anything has happened to her, I'll be running in the other direction, stopping just long enough to phone the police."

"Thanks," I replied dryly.

"Hey, don't thank me. You're the one who's a fifth-kyu aikido expert." She was referring to the test I'd taken to qualify for the lowest rank on the aikido totem pole.

"It's just a test for myself, not for competition," I muttered, not really believing myself. The philosophy of aikido is *Agatsu,* or, translated, Victory over Self. It's the one martial art that doesn't believe in competition, because the philosophy is as important as the physical aspect.

Cynthia's apartment was just a subway stop on my way home. I was still worried about her since Lisa Browning was murdered. I suspected that the driver who'd tried to run me down a few hours ago was acquainted with Lisa and might even be her killer. If the killer knew about me, I had to suspect that he or she knew about my client, and I had to make sure she was all right. Unless my client was the killer—then I would be walking right into a trap, and I would be bringing Raina along for the danger. But I'd already justified Cynthia's assault record. She was young, and probably assaulted the teacher because she didn't get an A on an exam.

Raina had already been with me at Lisa Browning's apartment, and if we'd gotten there first, she might have been in danger. If the killer tried for a third time tonight, he might get a three-for-one deal: Cynthia, me, and Raina. I tried to push that thought out of my head.

Raina and I arrived at the Hynes station and briskly walked the two blocks to Cynthia's apartment. She lived in a brownstone on Beacon, one that had a view of Cambridge, across the bay.

I went up to the vestibule and checked the names, found "C. MacDonald," and pressed the buzzer. No one answered.

"How far do you want to take this thing?" Raina asked, probably thinking I was ready to break and enter to satisfy my paranoia.

I frowned. "I don't know. She's not answering her phone or her doorbell, so most likely she's out." I shook my head, remembering Cynthia's juvenile record. "I'm sure I'm being stupid." I turned and headed across the street, intending to go back to the T station.

"Probably," Raina agreed cheerfully. "Let's go back to Eastie. I'm staying overnight, remember? That way—" she grinned "—I can consult with you on your wardrobe for tomorrow night." When we go out on a weeknight, Raina often stays overnight at my place because she lives in Waltham and her job is in East Boston.

I looked at her in a casual way. "I already know what I'm wearing tomorrow night."

"What?"

"My black fringed jacket."

Raina's eyes got big. "Oooh! And nothing else?"

We were on the other side of the street from my client's apartment and I was attempting to hit my best friend with my flattened purse when she stopped me and pointed across the street. "Is that her?"

I peered into the gloomy Boston night and saw Cynthia's bulky form walking up the steps alone.

She was wearing a black or dark blue raincoat and sweats underneath. Not the sort of fashion a girl wears for a night out on the town.

I thought about calling out, "Hi! We were just in the neighborhood and thought we'd look you up to make sure you hadn't killed anybody recently—" but something stopped me. Raina punched my arm playfully and I let out an involuntary "Ow!" My client had been about to go inside when she stopped and started to turn toward where Raina and I were standing. I pulled my friend deeper into the shadows. Maybe it was my imagination, or the ghostly effect of the streetlights, but Cynthia's face looked pale and worried to me.

I glanced at my watch—it was almost eleven-thirty. Enough time to get back from South Boston after killing someone. At this point I wasn't sure what to think.

When Cynthia was safely inside, Raina hit me again on the shoulder to get my attention.

"Ow. If you don't stop doing that," I told her, "I'll be forced to put you in a submission hold and march your butt down to the Hynes T station."

Raina, as usual, ignored my empty threats. "Why didn't you talk to her?"

"Why should I? I wanted to make sure she was safe, and she sure looked okay from this distance." We started walking toward the station.

"Yeah, she did. Angie, you gotta stop being so paranoid."

"Oh, right. Just because I'm paranoid, it doesn't

mean there isn't someone out to get me. My first case," I pointed out, "I get mugged and my client gets killed on the same night. This case, I almost get hit by a guy who seems to be aiming his car at me—and you're in the way, by the way—and so I naturally jump to the conclusion that my client might be in trouble." We reached the station and started down the steps.

"All you did was to find the woman who was impersonating her," Raina observed.

"Yeah, and now she's dead." We fed the turnstiles and went down to the platform heading toward Park Station. "So what does that tell you?"

Raina frowned, pulling at a strand of blond hair and twisting it around her finger. "That the two incidents tonight aren't necessarily related. For instance, if the guy who almost hit us was part of some conspiracy that involves Lisa Browning's murder, how did he know where you were?"

"He could have followed us."

Raina gave me a look that told me how improbable she thought that was.

"Well, it could have happened," I said in a defensive tone. Maybe it was improbable, but it wasn't impossible.

She rolled her eyes. "Yeah, and this supposed killer followed us to dinner and the movies, waiting almost four hours to make his move."

That silenced me. Maybe she was right. Maybe I *was* paranoid. On the other hand, the killer might have latched onto me while I was digging around trying to discover the source of my client's credit woes. It didn't seem to be something that was worth killing for, but I've seen plenty of cases where people killed for less reason. And I was uneasy about the fact that Cynthia wasn't at home when Lisa was murdered—just a few hours after I had given a report to my client that included the identity of the woman who had posed as her. Of course, I had problems with the idea of Cynthia trying to kill me; while I believed she was capable of it, there was no motivation there, unless she just didn't want to bother to pay my bill.

Raina and I discussed it all the way home. I pointed out that while Lisa Browning might not have been a bad person, the people with whom she probably hung around didn't take kindly to contact with the police.

Raina pointed out that true name fraud rings weren't into killing people. I shrugged and told her there was always a first time. When we fell silent, I started thinking about the scenarios that might have been—whoever had tried to run me over might have followed me from Lisa's apartment.

That was pretty much the end of that. We switched subjects to how the Celtics were going to do this season. I had hated to see the Boston Garden in the North End auctioned off piece by piece, but I had taken part in it. I bid a hundred dollars on a bag of dirt swept from the floor of the stands. It wasn't as much as the woman who paid three hundred for the *first* bag of Boston Garden dirt. I thought she was nuts, but of course a hundred bucks for dirt wouldn't keep me from being labeled certifiable either.

Raina and I spent about half an hour trying on my various clothes, all hanging in my closet by color and sleeve length. When she told me I had too much time on my hands and suggested I wear my fatigues to impress the guy, I hit her with a pillow and told her to go to bed.

TEN

ON FRIDAY MORNING, Raina and I quarreled over the use of the bathroom. She takes about an hour getting ready so she can sit on her butt all day, while I spend only ten minutes showering and making sure my hair doesn't have some major mat in it. I think the result is pretty much the same, except that she probably looks like she just stepped into a nice, fresh breeze as opposed to a steam room; her hair is nicely styled instead of damp and tousled, and her clothes always look carefully put together instead of thrown together. Not that I look that bad, but I'm not exactly ready to be on the cover of *Glamour*.

We finally compromised. She took a quick—for her—shower, then took my blow dryer into the bedroom while I got ready. When I was done, she came back in to put her makeup on. I hate makeup and use it only when I'm forced to get dressed up. I think I've had the same mascara wand for three years.

Before she left for work, Raina ultimately decided that if I *had* to wear the fringed leather jacket, I should wear Rosa's black-leather skirt with it and a pair of cowboy boots I'd picked up when I was stationed in Texas. I didn't tell her that I'd compromise—I'd wear the boots, but it was cold outside and no matter how many pairs of pantyhose I wore, the wind would reach up like a cold hand and grab parts of me that are meant to stay warm. Instead, I'd wear a pair of black jeans I'd recently picked up. But I thanked her before she left my apartment with a cinnamon-raisin bagel in her mouth and a commuter mug full of coffee.

I got dressed quickly, went to the office and picked up some material for the police. On the way out the door, I noticed that the answering machine was blinking, telling me I had several messages, but when I checked the number of messages, only my client's and the dead woman's messages were on the machine. I replayed Cynthia MacDonald's message to make sure she hadn't used her name. When I was satisfied that she couldn't be identified by the police, I replaced it with a new tape and put it in my purse. I hailed a cab and got to the South Boston precinct a little after the hour Sturgeon and I had agreed on.

The South Boston precinct was…well, like every other police station in Boston: an overworked, underpaid staff in a cheerless work environment that made the perps, the hookers, and the victims look even more unappealing than they were, if that were possible. There was no such thing as a "No Smoking" sign in the lobby, and the air was even worse when I got to the lieutenant's cubicle in the back.

Sturgeon was still out—it had been a late night for him, apparently—but I got his second-in-command, a female sergeant. She was a stunner, with dark, shoulder-length, naturally curly hair and cheekbones on which you could cut a ripe tomato.

She smiled with her mouth but not her eyes, and extended her hand, introducing herself as Sergeant Dana Proux. "Please sit down, Ms. Matelli." She pulled up her own chair to a computer, adjusted her reading glasses, and hit a couple of keys. "Full name?"

I told her.

"Address?"

I told her.

"Phone number where I can reach you both in the day and evening."

I recited the numbers. I'd gone over this with Sturgeon, but it wasn't surprising that I was going over it once more. By the time I left here, I probably would have verified my phone number, name, and address several more times.

"Occupation?"

I was beginning to feel as if I was in a personnel office, interviewing for a job instead of being questioned about my connection to a murder. "Private investigator."

She stopped typing and looked at me over her glasses. "You're the private investigator who was questioned by Lieutenant Sturgeon last night?"

I nodded.

She consulted a notepad with scribbling on it. "You are supposed to have brought some information with you regarding a case you're working on, something that might be pertinent to the victim's death."

I pulled out the sheaf of computer paper and

handed it to her. "This is all I can give you right now."

The sergeant scanned the pages of information on my case. I'd taken the liberty of blacking out my client's name and any other pertinent information that would lead to her. Sergeant Proux frowned. "This doesn't give us much to go on."

I shrugged. "I'm cooperating to the best of my ability, but I can't give you anything that would lead to my client's identity. Unless I turn up something that connects her to the murder."

I could tell she wasn't happy about it, but she nodded. She put the papers aside and stared at the monitor.

"Angela Matelli." Great. I was going to get the intimidation number. Sometimes cops will pull the "your name looks familiar—where have I seen it before?" If you have something in your background that you don't want anyone to find out about, this technique is supposed to make you sweat. Even though I didn't have anything to sweat over, my deodorant was working at maximum efficiency and still not getting the job done.

"Your last name seems familiar. Where have I seen it before?" She was asking herself, but I thought I'd try to help her along.

"Um, I'm a good friend of Lee Randolph at the Berkeley precinct." It wouldn't hurt to mention the names of the cops I was acquainted with.

It didn't impress her. She shook her head. "That doesn't ring a bell. I mean, I know his name from the roster, but I don't know him personally. Matelli. You aren't related to Maria Matelli, are you?"

I blinked. "Ma?"

Her eyes brightened. "You're her daughter? My father talks about her all the time, wondering whatever happened to her. I guess they used to date when they were in their early twenties. Before she married Vincent Matelli."

This was news to me. Ma as a young girl? Dating? I couldn't picture it. She'd always looked exactly the same to me: a sixtyish woman of small stature, hair kept carefully jet-black, a few wrinkles and liver spots, but always the same.

She divorced my dad about twenty years ago. Well, divorced is a strong word for a devout Catholic. Ma hadn't actually divorced him in the eyes of the church, but she hadn't lived with him for the last twenty years.

Dad lives in Malden as well, but he makes himself pretty scarce in the lives of his children. I think I see him about once a year, as an obligation. In the early days of my growing up, he'd been as good a dad as a married Italian guy could be. Ma always checked with him before buying shoes or clothes or anything out of the ordinary, but in an Italian household, the woman rules behind the curtain. For instance, if the kids need shoes for Easter, she will look at her budget and realize that yes, they had enough to afford new shoes for the kids. But before she goes out to buy the shoes, she'll go up to her husband and ask in a sly manner that leaves him no choice.

"Vince," Ma would say, "the kids need new shoes." Now this may seem simple, but you have to understand the way the guy's mind works—he might be thinking of using that money on the ponies or the dogs. But now he's faced with a decision— tell his wife to buy the shoes and when you go out in public, his wife can say, "Look at what Vince bought for his children—new shoes for Easter!" Now, if he chooses to gamble instead of looking out for the welfare of his children, he will still have to go out the next Sunday with his wife and children, and when people at Mass look pointedly at his children's old shoes, his wife will say, "We couldn't afford new Easter shoes this year. By the way, did you know that Old Hound won the seventh at Wonderland? I was hoping Bright Future would win."

Now the husband feels like the dog that lost the race. This is what went on for the first eight years of my life in our family. Toward the end, though, my dad began to gamble heavily and Ma couldn't stand it anymore. She knew that he was a bad influence on the children. One night she gave him an ultimatum: quit gambling, or leave the house for good. Dad is a proud man, but Ma is a strong woman, and she won out, but only by a hair. Dad left the house and continued to gamble, but he managed to send money back to care for the children.

It was pure luck that it hadn't affected me much, or Rosa, for that matter. But I sometimes wonder if that was why Sophia was so screwed up when it came to men, though lately she's been straightening out her act. As far as my brothers go, each one has taken a different path. Albert is secretive, Raymond is as straitlaced as they come, but Vince seems to take after the old man. He gambles. Not heavily, but enough for his first marriage to fail. He's on his second marriage, this time to Carla, and so far, it seems to be working.

"My father would love to see her again," Sergeant Proux said. "Any chance she's single again?"

I shrugged regretfully. "Ma hasn't lived with my dad for many years, but it's a Catholic divorce. You know the kind."

Dana Proux nodded sympathetically.

"But it doesn't mean they can't get together for old times' sake."

She smiled and shook her head. "He's still carrying a torch for her." She bent over some paperwork.

"Have you ever seen my mother?" I asked in as neutral a way as possible.

Without missing a beat, she replied, "Have you ever seen my father?" We exchanged photos. I keep photos of the family in my wallet. Ma's photo was taken last Christmas with the whole family, but I'd had the negative blown up so I had a nice one of just her and a little of Sophia's left shoulder.

"She's not bad-looking for a woman her age."

I suppressed a smile, studying her father's face. I could see a lot of his daughter in him. He was thin and had a face as sharp as a razor blade. But there was humor in his eyes and his smile. He looked a little like Fred Astaire, which wasn't such a bad thing. I liked him. I tried to picture the two of them together, Ma and the sergeant's father.

"What's his name?"

"George Proux."

I nodded and reluctantly handed the photo back to the sergeant. We smiled at each other, both of us probably thinking about getting two old flames together.

Then it was back to business. She seemed to feel more comfortable around me now that she knew I hadn't just come in one night and put up a sign to advertise that I was a private investigator. Somewhere between Ma and Dana's father, I'd become family. I answered all of her questions about why my client had hired me in the first place—I had no reason to hide that fact and I didn't want Dana Proux to think I was being uncooperative.

On the other hand, I did withhold information— while I gave Dana the tape of the message Lisa had left on my answering machine yesterday, I skipped the part about witnessing my client enter her apartment building at eleven-thirty last night. By the time I finished my statement, we were old friends.

She stood up and extended her hand. "Thank you for taking the time to come down, Angela."

"My pleasure. You have my number. Let's get my mother and your father together, okay?" I was thinking it would be nice for Ma to meet one of her old flames. She hadn't had a romance in so long, what would a little meeting hurt?

I felt pretty good when I left the precinct.

ELEVEN

I WENT TO LUNCH at one of my favorite delis, and while I waited for my order to come up, I used the pay phone to call my client. She wasn't at her office, or at home. I left messages at both places that I wanted to talk to her as soon as she got my message.

When I got back to the office, my sense of well-being disappeared upon finding Dana Proux waiting for me outside my door.

She gestured toward my locked door and the cheerful "Be back soon!" sign with the happy face on it. My niece Stephanie had picked it out for me for my last birthday.

"Nice to see you again, Sergeant," I said in a bright voice.

She didn't look happy to see me. "Ms. Matelli, we need to talk again. I just heard the tape and one of your messages mentioned the murder victim. I want to know the name of the woman who left the message and where I can find her so I can interview her."

"You could have left a message on my machine. I would have gotten back to you," I replied as I started to unlock my door. I opened the door and left it that way so she could follow me in. I picked up the mail that the building super delivers to our mail slots, and sat down at my desk to sort through it, trying to look casual.

Proux sat down in the client chair. "Yes, I could have. But this is a murder investigation, and I don't like the fact that you're playing fast and loose with the law."

I stopped pretending to look at my junk mail and looked up at her. "Is that what you think? I'm just doing this to irritate you and make your life more unbearable?"

She paused, as if she had to think about that one. "No, but I think that as a private investigator, your obligation to your client only goes so far. This woman was murdered and you have a connection to it. I think you can reveal the name of your client without many repercussions."

"What would you know about it?" I shot back. "My reputation is at stake, and I don't turn clients' private business over without consulting them first. Once I've reached my client, I'll let her know that I'm turning her name over to you, if she doesn't give me a satisfactory alibi."

Dana Proux gave me a highly amused, superior look. "So now you've become the arbiter of whose alibi is airtight?"

I stopped sorting my junk mail from my bills and looked up at her. "What's this all about? You don't have a suspect? Has the ex-husband given you an airtight alibi and now you're grasping at straws? You can't have run out of suspects so quickly that now you're down to some woman who's never met the victim until last night.''

"You were the one who called nine-one-one, and you were on the scene shortly after that," she replied. "I need to check out your story. All of it, including this mysterious client."

"Look, Sergeant. I just got back from giving you my statement at the police station and I find that you're waiting at my office door, ready to browbeat me about my statement. I didn't get enough sleep, and I have a lot of work to do. I'd like to help you, but I don't have that much to tell you at the moment. I got a message from the murder victim, called her back and heard someone break into her apartment and start to assault her. I called the police, then went over there because I was concerned. End of story."

"You're a private eye. What kind of work would you be doing for a woman client that would involve Lisa Browning's name? Were you checking out a romantic involvement? Possibly checking out Lisa Browning for the ex's girlfriend?"

But I was bright enough to pick up something. "Are you saying that the ex still isn't out of the woods? He might have killed Lisa to keep her from telling his current girlfriend something about his past? That's reaching, isn't it?"

She didn't nod, but said, "Tim Browning has an alibi—his girlfriend swears he was with her all night. You know, he still had a quarter of a mill whole life policy on her. We found the papers in her apartment."

I shook my head. "You're on the wrong block, Sergeant. I wasn't working for the ex or the ex's girlfriend. I wasn't even working for Lisa. I called her as a concerned friend. She was helping me with a case I was working on."

She stood up and flipped a card onto my desk. "If you think of anything else, give me a call." There were no warm words about my mother and her father getting together. I figured I'd blown it for Ma. I watched Proux leave and felt nothing but relief.

I sat back in my chair, feeling guilty about Lisa's death. Maybe if I'd checked my messages sooner, if I hadn't gone to the movie with Raina, if I hadn't taken a night off. But what was I, a doctor on call? I had business hours and if someone got themselves killed off hours, tough. Right?

I took a deep breath and let it out slowly, closing my eyes to try to remind myself that her death wasn't my fault. But the face that took shape in my mind was the young girl, Jessica. Now, thanks to me, she was without a mother. The only thing that made me feel less guilty was the fact that Jessica had been with the father. At least I wasn't responsible for two deaths.

But I had to wonder—Tim Browning had a huge insurance policy on his wife and now she was dead. Could he have done it? In a complete leap away from logic, I wondered if he could have been involved in the credit card scam. Maybe he'd set her up to take a fall, given her that credit card so he could have custody of Jessica.

I remembered standing outside my client's apartment building last night and watching her walk up to the door, her face pale and worried. What did she have to worry about? I needed to get in touch with her. She wasn't in when I called, but I left a message telling her to meet me at the Caffe Vittoria on Hanover Street in the North End at noon. I ended the message with the words, "Lisa Browning is dead and we need to talk. Don't blow me off."

That gave me enough time to go back to South Boston and talk to Ben Twomey. I remembered he'd said he was a neighbor, but there were a lot of buildings around. It wasn't difficult to find him, though. He was in the phone book and when I reached him, he told me he'd be there until he went out for lunch. I got the Bronco out of the garage and drove over there in less than half an hour. He answered the door, the music of The Chieftains wafting by him.

"Welcome to my humble abode. Can I get you something to drink?" He ushered me inside and closed the door. A tin whistle tripped up and down the scales of an Irish air while the hand-held drum, known as a "bodhran" in Gaelic, beat out a rhythm that seemed forced out of the earth. Twomey went over to a small liquor cabinet and opened it. I saw single malt Irish whiskeys and Guinness.

"Never chill a Guinness," he said as he brought out two stouts and opened them, pouring them into half-pint glasses. He handed me one. I realized I hadn't even agreed to have a drink. It was still morning, and I wasn't crazy about drinking before noon.

The air ended and a lament began. Twomey raised his glass. I followed his example.

"This is a lament called 'Brian Boru,' in honor of the most famous warrior king in Irish history. Let us make a toast to Lisa Browning in his honor."

I had no idea what King Brian had to do with Lisa Browning, but I clinked glasses with Twomey and drank of the dark, creamy room-temperature stout.

"It's a shame about my neighbor, it is," Ben Twomey said after the toast. "I'll miss her little girl Jessica."

"Did you know them well?" I asked.

He shook his head. "No, but we talked when we met on walks by the bay, or when she was coming back from grocery shopping."

"Do you know her ex-husband?"

Ben Twomey made a face. "That one's a loser. Lazy as a dog on a hot summer day. But he seems to dote on his daughter."

Chalk one up for Jessica. At least Daddy loves her, even if he might have killed Mommy.

"Did Lisa and her ex get along?"

"Mostly, although," Ben Twomey replied, "every time he came to pick up Jessica, they'd get into it over child support. By the time he would leave with Jessica, Lisa would look very upset."

"Do you think Tim Browning would be capable of killing his ex-wife?"

Twomey laughed. "I don't know what he would be capable of because I don't know him—only saw him from a distance, and only know what Lisa mentioned to me. But it seems to me that it would be too much trouble for him to kill anyone. Why do you ask?"

I saw no reason to keep it from him. It might loosen his tongue if there was something he was withholding from me, which I very much doubted. "Apparently he had a two-hundred-fifty-thousand-dollar life-insurance policy on his ex-wife."

Twomey raised his white, bushy eyebrows. "Well, that'll be a nice income for a while. Do I think he could have done it? In my opinion, Tim Browning is a coward and a weasel, but I don't see him as a murderer. He might have paid someone else to do it, but again, I don't really know him at all."

"Have you seen her with anyone else lately? Are there any friends she has here in Southie? Any place she frequents?"

Ben Twomey frowned in thought. "Well, yesterday afternoon, late in the day, I saw a stocky woman standing outside the apartment building. When Lisa came up to the building with grocery bags in her arms, the woman walked over and started talking to her. Lisa looked very upset. I thought the woman was going to hit her. Lisa's daughter called to her from across the street and the woman backed off." He looked almost apologetic. "I was going to ask Lisa if she was all right, but I was afraid she would see me as a busybody. She hurried inside with Jessica, and a few hours later…well, you know what happened.''

"Can you describe the woman for me?''

Ben Twomey described Cynthia MacDonald down to the wart on her nose. I wondered if he had been using binoculars. Bless the busybody, I thought.

I put my half-finished Guinness down. "Well, thank you for your time. You've been a big help. Is there someone else in the neighborhood who might have known Lisa well enough to talk to me?''

"No, like I said before, she moved in a few months ago and seemed to be struggling financially. She spent most of her days with her daughter, or working temp jobs when she could afford the time. No, what you want to do is go over there to the apartment this afternoon. Her mother will be coming to get a dress for her daughter and some clothes for Jessica.'' He paused, then added, "I only know this because I had coffee with Lisa's landlord this morning.''

I hadn't been planning to talk to Mrs. O'Connell, but she might be able to shed light on Lisa for me. I'd be able to talk to her and look around Lisa's apartment at the same time. Meantime, I had to meet my client for lunch in the North End. I locked the Bronco, left it parked on the street, and took a cab to the financial district. It would be impossible to ride all the way into the North End at the lunch hour, so I walked from there.

I was still feeling sorry for myself when I arrived

at the Caffe Vittoria, an upscale Italian restaurant-lounge. The managers of Caffe Vittoria like to bill their establishment as the "Original Italian Café"—who am I to argue? I haven't been to Italy yet, and I only know East Boston and the North End, and some of the Italian sections of other cities around the country.

I don't drink often, nothing stronger than wine or beer, now that I'm out of the service, but today was an exception. I ordered a Jim Beam, straight up. Was I responsible for what my client might have done?

And what about Lisa Browning—had I gotten her killed?

I stopped with one drink. I can drink several beers or glasses of wine without much effect, but hard liquor goes straight to my center of balance and reason. By the time I was on my second espresso, Cynthia arrived. She looked put out, but I ignored the pout and nodded to her.

"I was in a meeting with a client when your call came through. This is really annoying."

I was puzzled. "What's annoying?"

"This woman is dead," she said in a tone that suggested I was a moron. "How am I ever going to clear up my credit?"

I stared at her.

"What?" she asked.

"I just talked to a witness who saw you outside of Lisa Browning's apartment yesterday afternoon about five-thirty or six."

She avoided my eyes. "I don't know what you're talking about."

A waiter interrupted us to take our orders. I got the pasta fagioli and salad. I could tell she was distracted because she told the waiter to bring her whatever the special was for the day.

"Ms. MacDonald, if I know about you, the police are going to find you sooner or later, and their questions will be tougher than mine."

She looked me in the eye. "I went there to see what kind of woman would do this to another person. She panicked and ran into the house. She wouldn't stay and talk to me. I got mad because I wanted to settle this thing once and for all. I thought maybe if I talked to her—"

"So what were you doing between six o'clock and ten-thirty?" I asked.

She didn't look at me. "I went to a movie. I was upset, I thought maybe if I just go see Tom Cruise in something and take my mind off —" She took out a cigarette and lit it, took a deep drag, and let it out. It was a good thing I'd taken a table in the smoking section.

"How about saying all of that with more conviction? You look like you're lying."

She gave me a sharp look, then softened a bit. "Angela, I didn't kill her. I swear I didn't. It wouldn't make any sense. I needed her alive to bring her to the police to clear up my credit."

Even if she didn't seem sincere about her alibi, her reason for not killing Lisa Browning rang true to me. Committing murder wasn't the sensible thing to do because it would cause my client more problems than it would solve. And if there was one thing I could say about Cynthia MacDonald, she was cutthroat enough to do what needed to be done to make her life better. I had no doubt that if killing Lisa Browning would have served her purposes, she would have done it.

I leaned forward. "You know, Cynthia, I can check on your car, when you brought it back, whether you took it out of the garage a second time last night."

She ground out her cigarette and sat back. "That wouldn't prove anything."

"It would prove to my satisfaction that you didn't go to that Tom Cruise movie, because you'd take the subway to see a movie." It was time to play one of my cards.

"I happened to have walked past your place last night to see if you were all right. And that was at eleven-thirty. You were just coming home."

She didn't react at first. Then a full blush crept up from her neck to her forehead. "I ran out to get some ice cream."

She shook her head as if she was reading my thoughts. "I wasn't in South Boston again, if that's what you're worried about."

Okay, she wasn't going to tell me where she'd been, but she all but admitted that she'd been lying earlier. And I was pretty sure she was lying to me now.

I leaned over and said in a low voice, "Before this case is over, I will know where you were last night. That's the sort of thing I'm hired to do, and I'm damned good at it."

A look flitted across Cynthia's face—it was so brief, I couldn't tell if it was fear or just something secretive. She looked me straight in the eyes. "I went to a movie. I got home about ten-thirty. The only thing I neglected to mention is that later I went down to the local all-night store and got a carton of ice cream."

That was interesting, because I didn't recall seeing her carrying a bag. I didn't point it out though, deciding to save it for later. When I didn't reply, it bothered her enough to continue talking. "I mean, it was one of those big hits. I think it was a Tom Cruise movie. I was distracted by my confrontation with Lisa, so I wasn't really paying attention."

"What theater?"

"Um, somewhere downtown near the Common. I can't tell one theater from another down there." She was fidgeting, and sweat had broken out on her already shiny forehead. My client wasn't a good liar. I wondered what she was keeping from me. Why not tell the investigator, who's on your side? Either she did kill Lisa or there was something she didn't want anyone to know—like a meeting with some person, or at some place, that she didn't want to be associated with on this case. What could be so important that she couldn't tell me where she'd really been?

"Where's the stub? Did anyone see you go into the movie? Come out?"

She started to panic. "Why are you asking me all this? You're supposed to believe I'm innocent. I don't know where the stub is. I probably threw it away. And who would remember me? It's a big theater." Her voice became increasingly strident with each sentence.

I stood up and laid some money down to pay for my meal. "When you decide to tell me the truth, give me a call."

I WENT BACK to South Boston and caught Mrs. O'Connell as she was trying to fit a key in the door. A policeman accompanied her. She was a frail woman in her late fifties, early sixties. Men might call her handsome. Her hair was cropped short and curled in an old-fashioned style, and although she took care of it, she didn't bother to color it. Gray was liberally flecked throughout the faded red curls. She looked up at me, the pain of losing her daughter in such a hideous way was still bright in her eyes. The officer touched her arm and she looked at him dully. "Ma'am, I'm going to give you time to gather the things you'll need for your granddaughter. I'm going to wait outside."

I could smell cigarette smoke on him, and knew why he was leaving the scene of the crime. Mrs. O'Connell nodded. He turned to me and said, "Just don't touch anything in the living room. That's where she was, well, you know." He trailed off and backed himself down the stairs, clearly uncomfortable with the palpable grief.

It wasn't until he left that I realized he thought I was a relative who'd come to meet and support Lisa's mother. I felt slightly guilty, but I took advantage of the opportunity.

I introduced myself to her.

"Look, Mrs. O'Connell—"

"Call me Helen," she said as we climbed the stairs to the apartment.

"Okay. Look, Helen, I don't want to mislead you. I'm involved here because your daughter was involved with a credit-card fraud ring."

She stopped at the top of the stairs and turned to face me. "Oh, that can't be true. Lisa was a good girl."

I closed my eyes. I'd probably blown it. But I plowed ahead. "I don't think she was directly involved, but she knew someone who was part of the ring. And she used someone's credit to buy some luxury items for her daughter and herself. And the person whose identity she used hired me to investigate. And Lisa got caught in my net."

Helen O'Connell's hand fluttered up to her breast and she leaned against the wall. She didn't look like she'd survive what I'd just told her. "I'd appreciate it if you'd leave now, Ms. Matelli."

"Please, Mrs. O'Connell," I replied. "I'm begging you to listen to me. I think your daughter was killed because she knew these people. She was about to give their names to me. I want to find your daughter's killer.''

Tears slid down her face and she turned away from me for a moment, fumbling in her small pocketbook for a handkerchief. She dabbed at her face, straightened her skirt, then turned back to me. "Please, won't you come in?"

The apartment smelled of orange juice and stale milk. As I walked through the living room to the kitchen to get a glass of water that Lisa Browning's mother had requested, I noticed that the television and VCR were gone. I could also see—despite some scrubbing—the bloodstains where Lisa had been bludgeoned to death.

In the kitchen, a pan of dried oatmeal sat on one of the burners. It looked like it had been there a few days. Dirty dishes sat in a pool of cold, soapy water in the sink, the product of good intentions and not enough time. I got a clean glass, filled it from the tap, and took it into the living room. Mrs. O'Connell was seated on the sofa, staring at the wall. "I don't know what I'm going to do."

"I'm sorry about the television and VCR," I said.

"What do you mean?" she asked after taking a sip of the tepid water.

"When I talked to the police, they told me it was assumed that the items had been stolen."

"No," she replied. "Lisa called me yesterday afternoon and asked if she could bring some things over to my house, in Dorchester. I was surprised to see a brand-new television and the tape machine, but they would have been nice to have. I'll return them this week.'' She looked down. ''I'm sorry. I didn't know they were—what's the word I'm looking for—contraband?''

I felt sorry for her. ''You couldn't have known. And she just wanted to make you happy. I'm sorry I had to tell you.''

Mrs. O'Connell got up and began sorting through Jessica's toys, carefully avoiding the area where Lisa had been killed. ''Well, you'll have to give me the name and address of the store where she bought them and I'll return them.''

I walked over to the television stand to pick up a toy, and the answering machine caught my eye. Looking over, I could see that Mrs. O'Connell had her back turned to me. I looked in the machine and saw that the tape was still there. I slipped it into my pocket, then turned the machine over and memorized the serial number on the back.

''So you're looking for someone who might have been connected to a fraud ring. If you're looking at Tim Browning, you've got the wrong man. He's too lazy to get involved in anything that would require work. And this sounds like it's more work than he'd be interested in doing.'' She turned to look at me and smiled wanly. ''He's not a bad father, he loves Jessica dearly and she adores him. But he's a lousy provider.''

''What's going to happen to Jessica?''

She sat back on her heels and sighed. ''I talked to Tim this morning and he wants me to take my granddaughter. I'm happy to do so, but I know his mother will put up quite a fuss.''

"When I talked to Lisa, she mentioned her mother-in-law. She sounds like a dragon.''

Helen nodded. ''Yes, that's a good way of putting it. Even Tim has gotten to the point where her overbearing manner bothers him. She's well-meaning, but she doesn't think about the feelings of others.''

I changed the subject slightly. "Did you ever meet a friend or love interest of Lisa's, someone you might not have had a good feeling about?''

Mrs. O'Connell shook her head. ''No, not lately.''

"What about someone named Spence? She mentioned a Spence when we spoke one time.''

Lisa's mother stopped what she was doing. ''I think I remember that name from somewhere, but I can't recall.'' She tried to think, but finally shook her head again.

"Okay, what about love interests? Were there any men she might have been seeing?''

Mrs. O'Connell's expression brightened. ''She brought one fellow to dinner recently, I felt so sorry for him. He'll never amount to much, it's so clear. I don't know why she's attracted to losers.'' There was that word again—loser. Ben Twomey had used it when describing Tim Browning. Lisa had a thing for losers.

"Do you remember anything about him?''

"Sure. He's crazy about her. A nice young man, but I don't think he'll get far in life.''

"Why do you say that?'' I asked.

"I think he's twenty-nine or thirty years old and still working as a salesclerk for a chain of stores that sells TVs and computers. He doesn't seem to have any ambition to move up."

I was getting a feeling…I was close to something. "What's his name?"

"Jimmy. Jimmy Stiles."

The name rang a bell. A big bell. A Tech City bell.

TWELVE

BEFORE I LEFT, Helen O'Connell gave me Tim Browning's address and phone number, but I wasn't as interested in talking to him now that I had Jimmy Stiles. I had already seen a red flag in his financial statements—all that money for a guy who worked full-time at Tech City as a salesclerk. But I hadn't had any reason to suspect that Jimmy Stiles was part of a credit-fraud ring. Now, looking back on the money in his bank account and at the sports car, it made sense to me. There *was* a connection.

I went back to the office and phoned Sergeant Proux. At least I had something to give her. She wasn't in, so I went through voice mail hell to leave her a message. Then I turned back to the problem at hand—what do I do next? It seemed that a visit to Tim Browning would be in order. Jimmy Stiles was a good possibility for Lisa's murder, and the police would be handling that, but I wanted to see the man who would benefit by a quarter of a million dollars from his dead ex-wife.

I picked up my Bronco from where I'd left it and drove by Tim's apartment in South Boston. He lived only a couple of blocks from his ex-wife, probably as a convenience for seeing his kid.

Tim was home, which wasn't a surprise considering that he wasn't working. He met me at the door, a short, skinny man with bad skin, wearing an off-white T-shirt and jeans. I found it hard to believe that this was Jessica's father. And it was hard for me to picture Lisa with this man.

After I introduced myself, he let me in. Jessica wasn't there. The living room was done in typical bachelor decor, with lots of browns and plaids. Everything was secondhand except for the big-screen TV that sat in the middle of the room. A sports cable channel was on at the moment. I wondered how a man in Tim's unemployed position had gotten a television that nice.

"Where's your daughter?" I asked, looking around.

He seemed surprised that I knew Jessica. "She's with my mother. Uh, are you here to give me my money? I already went to the insurance company and filled out some forms." He sat down in a secondhand easy chair. I perched on the sofa. None of it looked too sanitary. I was ready to call in the Health Department.

"No, I'm here on an entirely different matter." I already didn't like him, but it wasn't that Tim Browning was evil, he was just stupid and greedy. Here his ex-wife was lying in a morgue somewhere, barely twenty-four hours dead, and he's wanting his money. I certainly wasn't going to tell him about his ex-wife's problems with the law. I wondered what she'd seen in him. Had he always been this way, or had it been a gradual dumbing down?

I could smell the alcohol on his breath and it explained some of his problem.

"Well, I'll answer your questions, as long as you don't get too personal." He winked at me. "You want a beer?"

"No, thanks. I'm not allowed to drink on the job." I started with the alibi. "Where were you last night?"

"My daughter Jessica can tell you I was with her all night long." He said this with a grin. I guessed it was something he was proud of. I found it odd that this lazy drunk actually had feelings for his little girl. I wandered over to peer at a couple of framed pictures sitting on a table. One was of Lisa and a man who was the Before version of Tim Browning. He was clear-eyed, looked happy to be getting married, and had one of those late-'80s hairstyles that afflicted a lot of men back then.

"What do you know of your ex-wife's activities? Was she seeing anyone?"

"She just took care of Jessica," Tim said before taking a pull on his beer bottle. "I don't think she ever dated after we got divorced."

"How come there was a policy on your wife that was still in your name?"

He shrugged. "We bought and paid for them a long time ago. Guess we both forgot about them."

"It seems to me that she would want that money to go to her daughter, your daughter, not her ex-husband."

Tim Browning looked uncomfortable. "Yeah,

well, Jessica's gonna get her share. I'm not a dead-beat dad, you know.''

That brought me to another subject, one I brought up just to be nasty. ''Speaking of deadbeat, I heard from Lisa that you weren't real regular with the child support.''

He squirmed in his seat. ''Hey, what is this? Who are you anyway?''

I shrugged casually. ''I can always find out why from other sources.''

I'd hit a nerve. ''It's always been a sore spot with me. But you see, I got this bum knee at work a few years ago and they laid me off because I couldn't go back on the job. And the union backed them up. My doctor wouldn't back me when I told him I needed more time off to recover, so I'm on worker's comp now.''

''I see.'' And I did see. This was a guy who couldn't kill his wife because he was too lazy. And he probably couldn't even get up enough energy to find someone else to do the job for him. But in the end, Tim Browning didn't seem to be the type of guy who would even think about doing something like that.

''So tell me, Tim,'' I said as I sat down across from him, ''how come a guy like you who obviously loves his daughter isn't willing to take care of her? You're letting your mother-in-law be her guardian, I understand.''

Tim Browning actually sobered up for a moment. Then he looked me in the eyes. ''You have to understand," he replied, "I love my daughter. I have this girlfriend, Doreen, who isn't real good with children. I just think Jessica'd be better off with Helen than with me. I'll still be part of her life—" He trailed off and stared into space.

I was actually quite touched that he was making a sacrifice. It was clear he loved his daughter—there was the one photo of Lisa and Tim when they were getting married, then the rest of the pictures were of Jessica as a baby, a toddler, and so on. He did love his daughter, and it was hard to reconcile the man I was talking to with the loving father he seemed to be as well.

"Have you ever heard your wife mention someone named Spence?"

He thought about it for all of three seconds, about the length of his attention span. "Nah. Can't say that I have. Of course, there could be a dozen Spences in her life and I wouldn't know it. All's we did those last few months was argue over those damn child support payments. I don't know what she expected me to do."

The obvious answer—get a job—sailed past his head. I had one more question to ask before I left.

"How did you end up with such a large insurance policy?"

He seemed surprised that I'd even ask. "Lisa and me, we took it out on each other when we first got married. To take care of Jessica if anything should happen to one or both of us." He looked toward the picture of the two of them. "It was sure a good thing that Lisa insisted on that policy. It'll sure come in handy.''

IT WAS CLOSE TO FIVE, so I went straight home. A dark blue Mercury was parked right outside my building, and as I came up to the door, a woman got out of the driver's side. It was Dana Proux.

I stopped and gave her a stony stare. "You planning to stalk me now?"

She shrugged. "Nope. Thought I'd come by and see if you know where Jimmy Stiles is. Seems he's dropped off the face of the earth."

I smirked and crossed my arms. "That's what my office is for. My hours are the same as for most businesses."

"Look, I want to work with you," she said. "I think we've both got some valuable information and we may be able to solve this case if we pool our resources." I was about to tell her to go take a hike when she added, "Besides, I think this case is bothering you as much as it bothers me."

Even though I didn't like Cynthia, I had liked Lisa despite the fact that she'd made a mistake. From our one conversation, I had the impression that she was a little bit naive, and that someone who knew her had given her the credit to "buy" the items she had in her apartment. But I wasn't convinced that that someone, possibly Jimmy, had killed her. The name "Spence" nagged at me. Whoever Spence was, he was good at eluding me and everyone else in Lisa's life.

I resolved to find Jimmy tomorrow and talk to him.

I narrowed my eyes and gave Dana a sidelong glance. "Oh, you're good," I said. "You hit me in the soft spot." Jessica, Lisa's kid. Yeah, I wanted to solve this case just for her.

She touched my elbow hesitantly and gestured to her car. "You wanna grab some dinner and we can talk about this?"

I did have a blind date with a doctor to look forward to. I could show up with Dana on my arm. Nah, that wouldn't work. Might scare Dr. Reginald off. Of course, maybe scaring Dr. Reginald off might be the best thing I could do.

"Look, I've got this date with this doctor—"

Dana crossed her arms and grinned. "Oh, I understand."

I shook my head. "No, I don't think you do. Ma set this blind date up for me."

Dana's grin grew wider and her eyes sparkled. If I was a man, I'd have gone for her in a minute. But I didn't lean that way. "Then I definitely do understand. My mother set me up on a few blind dates when I was single."

"Yeah? Hey, why don't you come up to my place for a drink while I get ready for my big date."

She agreed.

Dana made herself at home in my living room. She had a glass of wine in one hand, a Lyle Lovett CD was softly playing in the background—and she was peering at Fredd, my watch iguana, through the glass aquarium. Fredd was peering back, his head cocked at a curious angle. Of course, Fredd's head was cocked at a curious angle a lot of the time. I walked over and filled his bowl with alfalfa pellets and made sure he had enough water.

Dana turned to me. "What is he?"

"An iguana," I told her.

"Most women I know have cats or fluffy little dogs," she said, giving Fredd one last look before crossing the living room to sit on my '50s boomerang-shaped sofa. I'd picked it up at an estate sale, along with matching easy chairs and a cool kidney-shaped coffee table.

"So, based on my gender, you figured me for the cat type?"

She shrugged and took a sip of her wine. "Most female private eyes in books have cats. Some have dogs."

"Do I look like I belong in a novel?" I asked, gesturing around the room. "This is my life, Dana. Stop romanticizing about the female PIs you know from books." I wondered which fictional PI she read the most. Kinsey? Sharon McCone? Stephanie Plum? I walked into the kitchen to get myself a glass of wine.

I said nothing, just waited. I glanced out into the living room and saw her looking at me in an openly curious manner.

The phone rang and I answered it.

"Angie?" I was getting to know the sound of Reginald's voice.

"Yeah. Let me guess. You've been called in again."

He groaned. "Yeah. Sorry about that."

"Look, Reginald, you know and I know that our mothers are behind this whole thing. Let's not make such a big deal about going out, okay? Call me when you're free and if I'm free, we'll meet. Otherwise, good luck with your internship."

He laughed. "You're refreshing. Very straightforward. I like that."

"You and my best friend," I replied, warming up to him a bit, even though I was sure he would turn out to be a troll. "Ma doesn't think I'm ladylike."

Dana laughed in the background. I glared at her to keep quiet and she tried to.

"Who was that?" Reginald asked.

"Someone who came over to my apartment to discuss a case with me."

Dana looked at me and gave me a mock frown. I shrugged helplessly. Reginald apologized once again and we hung up with promises to get together soon.

I turned back to Dana. "I guess I'm free tonight if you want to get something to eat."

She drained her glass and set it down. "Sounds good. Let's go. We can talk about the case."

I stopped her before she headed for the door. "Why are you doing this? It's an open case. PIs have to wait until a case is closed to work it."

She ran a hand through her mass of curls. I just knew it was natural, but I couldn't hate her for it.

"You sort of stumbled on the case, and I believe you've been straight with me so far. After I saw that little girl without a mother, I guess I just want the case solved as fast as possible. And I don't think my partner, Sturgeon, is going to solve it. He's just not interested enough. In fact, he told me today that if we didn't pick someone up, anyone, for the murder by the end of the week, he thought it should be filed as unsolved."

"It was a particularly vicious murder, from what he told me." I shuddered, recalling Lisa's pleas and the background noise of someone beating her.

Dana seemed sensitive to my reaction and put my mind on another topic, one close to my heart—food.

When she mentioned Greek, my knees went weak. Some women have an erogenous zone in the back of a knee or on the inside of a wrist. Take me to a good Greek restaurant and I'm yours forever.

THIRTEEN

DANA CERTAINLY KNEW her way to this girl's heart. She just didn't know when to quit. I was in the middle of enjoying a savory pastitsio at the wonderful little Greek place near the marina, when she began to talk business.

"I think the way we have to tackle this is—"

I held up my hand, too busy swallowing the combination of elbow macaroni, tomato sauce, cinnamon, ground lamb, Romano, and a custard sauce. "Let me eat in peace. This was supposed to be a relaxing night with a date, and instead, I'm sitting in a Greek restaurant with homicide detective jabbering in my ear about business."

She eyed me as if I were a hungry coyote, which wasn't too far from the truth—I was starving—and she went back to her Greek chicken. It was a nice dish—I'd had it here once before—but Dana obviously knew nothing about Greek food or she'd have ordered the moussaka or the stuffed grape leaves and pilaf. At least she'd had the decency to order a Greek salad, with the tart vinegar dressing laden with real basil and lots of feta. Heaven.

By the time I was done with my main course, Dana was staring at me as if I'd won a pie-eating contest.

"Are you finished?" she asked.

The waiter came around. I smiled up at him and ordered coffee and baklava.

Dana shook her head and ticked off every item I'd eaten. "You started with the egg lemon soup, plowed your way through a Greek side salad, then ate a meal of pastitsio and pilaf. Now you're ordering dessert and coffee?"

"You forgot the ouzo. I had two of those." I smiled as the waiter brought me my coffee and assured me that my dessert was on the way.

"Where the hell do you put it all? You're tiny! I have to watch every calorie or I'll blow up like one of the Teletubbies!"

I sipped my coffee, strong and black and hot. I shrugged. "What can I say? Investigation's a hungry business. Shall we get down to it? You've obviously interviewed the ex. So did I. Let's compare notes. What does he have to say for himself?"

"He didn't do it."

"Of course he says that. Were you able to prove it one way or the other?"

Dana frowned. "His girlfriend, Doreen, swears he was with her all night long. So was Jessica. We've talked to the daughter and she confirms it."

I made a face. "How sweet. Tim and his little impressionable daughter Jessica got to spend the night at a friend's house. I'm sure Lisa would have been happy to have heard that. What about boyfriends? Was Tim able to tell you anything about his ex-wife's life?"

Dana shook her head. It looked as if all I was going to get out of this meeting was a great meal. "He said she kept mostly to herself and was practically a virgin after the divorce."

I rolled my eyes. Why do most guys assume that once the divorce is final, the ex-wife doesn't have a sex life? My guess was that, unlike Tim, Lisa just didn't bring her love life home with her. She didn't want to confuse Jessica.

Dana asked a question. "What have you found out?"

"Pretty much the same thing. Except I didn't get a chance to interview the girlfriend. Was there any possibility she was lying?"

"No. She seemed to be a straight arrow. I think she's a replacement Lisa. Seems to have a decent job, seems responsible, and she's divorced once." She leaned back in her chair and looked at me. "You got anything else?"

I told her about Spence. "It's a little thing, but it bothers me. No one seems to know this Spence. I'm going to try to find Stiles tomorrow."

"He's gone underground. You think he has something to do with this credit-card ring you're after?"

I smiled. "I think he's the key to the whole damn moussaka."

"Doesn't seem like you have much to go on."

I grinned, figuring that since we were unofficially working together, it wouldn't hurt to let her have a little information. "For one thing, I have the serial number of the answering machine that was in Lisa's apartment.''

"So what? That's news for you, but it doesn't do me any good."

I explained that I had some information to verify that the answering machine was the same one that Lisa bought at Technology Bytes. I brought something out of my jacket pocket. "And I have the tape from the answering machine."

Dana looked outraged. She started to reach for it. "Where the hell did you get that? That's police property." Suddenly we took an official turn.

I held it away from her hand. "Ah, ah, ah. I'm just borrowing it. The crime scene unit was probably a little sloppy. As soon as I have a chance to listen to it, you can have it for evidence." I got serious. "Listen, Dana, you've got to trust me if we're going to work together on this case unofficially. But clear something up for me, please."

She made an effort to calm down. "What's that?"

"I still don't understand why Sturgeon is ready to give up on this case so quickly."

Dana looked down at the remains on her plate. "Sometimes good cops just stop doing everything they should do to close a case. He's getting toward retirement and I think Sturgeon had gotten to the point where he wants to do the minimum. He's decided that the victim was brutally beaten by a jealous lover, and he'll try to pin it on someone. But he's not trying very hard. And this case got to me."

"And you're willing to jeopardize your career to

see that Lisa Browning gets justice?" I asked. I wanted to know what made Dana Proux tick before I gave up any more information. I still found it hard to trust her, even if she made herself out to be a rogue cop. "I wouldn't want to do anything to jeopardize the police investigation. Lee Randolph will tell you that."

"I did call him. He said you're good at what you do and you care," she replied. "And your investigation methods might yield some information I can't get because my hands are tied by procedure."

I slipped the tape back into my pocket.

"Why are you being so belligerent with me?"

I smiled. "Because you went 'cop' on me all of a sudden and you haven't given me squat. Except for some great food. But it's not worth the price of admission."

Her tone was defensive. "You were so ravenous I thought you'd start gnawing on my arm if I didn't feed you. And I gave you what we have."

"And it's flimsy, Dana. Nothing I didn't already know," I said, taking a sip of tepid coffee. "Look, I don't want to beat you up or anything, and I'll be happy to work with you on the case, but if you need information, I'd rather you just come out and ask me instead of playing like you're gonna cut me in on a deal."

There was a lull as I took the opportunity to finish my baklava and drain my coffee cup before the waiter appeared beside me to refill it. I figured I'd be working pretty hard this weekend and I'd need all the caffeine I could handle.

Dana finally spoke. "I just hate to see a life unfinished. I guess it gets to me—a young woman killed, a kid motherless. I mean, I got a nephew about her age and he's living with his father. But my brother is an alcoholic and doesn't seem to know what to do with the boy."

"Where's the mother?"

Dana shrugged and looked down at her fingernails. "She took off. Couldn't handle the pressure of motherhood. I just feel so sorry for Eddie. It's not much of a life."

"Hey, Dana, he's got you. A lot of kids grow up with irresponsible parents and they turn out just fine because they were able to latch onto the one person in their life who cared. And that person is you, Dana. There's nothing wrong with being a good role model."

She looked down and nodded slightly, a little smile on her face. When she looked back up at me, she said, "You're okay, Angie."

I had to take a deep breath. We had work to do. "Yeah, you're okay, too, Dana. Let's find the bastard who cheated Jessica out of her mom."

She paid the bill and drove me back home. With her car still idling outside my apartment building, she reached into the backseat and pulled her briefcase up front. She dug around inside, and came up with two little black boxes. On close examination, I saw that one was a beeper and the other a cell phone.

"We can stay in touch with these." Geez, she'd thought this whole "unofficial" thing through.

I gingerly took them, a reminder that I wasn't completely up to date with all the latest gadgets. I could get a cell phone or beeper any time I wanted, for wholesale instead of retail, but I'd been resisting it. The idea that I would be at everyone's disposal twenty-four hours a day just didn't appeal to me. Hell, under duress, I'd just had a second line installed at the office, and call-waiting at home last month because I realized that every time Ma or Sophia called me at work to alert me to the latest gossip on the family, there might be a prospective client or two trying to reach me and giving up when they got a busy signal.

"Why would I need these?" I asked, holding the cell phone between two fingers as if it might contaminate me.

Dana grinned. "Ah, you're resistant to the idea of being at my beck and call."

I gave her a stony look. "I'm resistant to the cell phone and beeper in general."

Her smile disappeared. "Well, this is temporary. Just until this case is solved."

I shrugged my shoulders and stuffed the phone and beeper in my bag. "Whatever you say. It's your dime." I pulled the tape out of my pocket and shoved it into her tape deck. "We might as well listen to this now."

Beeeep. "Lisa? Jimmy. Just called to let you

know I'll pick you up tomorrow at six. And we'll talk about what's bothering you." Click.

Beeeep. "This is Spence. I hear you've been talking. I'll call back." Click.

And that was it for the tape.

The second voice sounded familiar. I'd heard it within the last few days, but I couldn't place it. I ejected the tape and gave it to Dana. "Not much help."

"No," she agreed. But I noticed she bagged it and would probably tag it later.

Dana gave me the number of my cell phone, her cell phone, and her beeper number. As I got out of the car, she made me promise to call with an update tomorrow. I couldn't imagine breaking a case that quickly, and I still wasn't completely confident with her reasons—beyond finding out if Tim Browning had done in his ex-wife.

Back in my apartment, the glow from our intimate moment had worn off and I started to think hard about Dana Proux. Was she just a benign homicide detective, or was there something more there?

But I liked her. Maybe after the case was wrapped up, we'd get to know each other. I hadn't seen much of anyone but Raina for a couple of months, not even the elusive Dr. Reginald. It was too bad Dana was female—we got along so well. And the closest I'd come to anything male was Fredd. At least cooking and cleaning for Fredd wasn't difficult. A few branches to climb on, a few pellets and vegetables to eat, water, a little sun or a reasonable facsimile, and he's happy. I wish all relationships were that easy.

Although tomorrow was Saturday, I set my alarm for seven and crawled into bed. It must have been a few hours later, probably close to six, when I heard the sound of a car motor rumbling outside my apartment building. It idled there for a long time, and I finally got out of bed to see what was going on. I stumbled and felt around for my robe, then stubbed my foot on something and let out a yell.

"Ow! Owowowowow," I said, nursing my foot.

I hopped to the window and looked out. A dark figure was getting out of the car's passenger side and entering the building.

It didn't seem possible that it was Rosa—she never stayed out this late. Sophia was staying with Dave, even though most of her stuff was still in the ground-floor apartment.

So it was only Rosa and me. I thought of Rosa, asleep through all this. I dialed her number to wake her up. Her phone kept on ringing. The front door had already creaked open and been shut quietly. I heard footsteps on the stairs, pausing occasionally.

I took a baseball bat from my front closet and grabbed the keys to Rosa's apartment. If this was the guy who'd tried to run me down, I wanted to confront him on my own terms. I had visions of the attacker getting into Rosa's apartment instead of mine, dragging her out and abducting her.

I took the stairs two at a time on the way down, intent on making as much noise as possible. When I sensed the person was nearby, I let out a yell, and swung the bat back, ready to strike.

FOURTEEN

THE FIGURE in front of me screamed and put its arms up in defense.

I put the bat down. "Rosa," I said. My heart was still racing. She slumped back, grabbing the railing for support.

"What the hell's the matter with you, Sarge?"

I took a deep breath. I tried to say something, but nothing came out.

She took my arm and steered me into her apartment, then made me sit on the sofa while she made tea. It was just getting light out. I looked at her living-room clock, a beautiful old deco alarm clock on a waterfall nightstand that stood next to her futon sofa. It was six o'clock.

The kettle whistled and a moment later, Rosa came into the living room with a couple of mugs of steaming peppermint tea. I gave her an edited version of what had happened over the past few days. When I finished, she was shaking her head.

"You could've been killed," she said, referring to the car that had almost made me one with the street. Her mug clattered on the coffee table. I noticed that her hand was shaking, and she leaned over and hugged me. "And tonight—"

I patted her back. She was more upset than I was at this point.

"Take it easy, Sis," I said. "I'm just glad we're both okay. I could have knocked your block off."

So far, there hadn't been any more attempts to get to me. But that made me even more nervous, because I was starting to see the bigger picture. It was only a matter of time before someone got edgy again and tried to put me out of commission.

"I'd better get ready," I told Rosa. "I have a big day ahead of me." I opened Rosa's door, then stopped as a thought occurred to me. "By the way, why were you coming in at this hour of the morning?"

She blushed and looked away. "Uh, I was at the museum."

I gawked. "What're you talking about? It doesn't open—"

She looked at me. "With someone else."

I did a double take.

"His name is Harrison and he's a security guard at the museum at night. I stop by at the end of his shift and we go out to breakfast," Rosa explained.

I grinned. "Sounds serious if you're willing to get up that early to see him."

Her dimple showed when she smiled back. "He's nice."

Another thought occurred to me. "Uh, look, Rosa, I hate to kick you out of your apartment, but if you could find some place to go for a little while—"

"Sarge," she replied in a severe tone, "I don't want to leave you alone."

"I'd feel better if I was worried only about myself instead of both of us."

She thought about it for a little while. "Harrison has his own place. He's gone at night. He'd probably let me use it."

I breathed a sigh of relief. "Good."

BACK AT MY APARTMENT, I looked up Jimmy's address, and his parents' address just to be on safe side, on Skip's background information. I was pretty sure that Jimmy wasn't going to work, since he'd made himself scarce with the police, but I figured he wouldn't be running too far from home base. I cruised by Jimmy's apartment just on the outside chance that he'd come home. There didn't seem to be any off-street parking, and I didn't see his Miata out front, which didn't say much for outside chances. That didn't mean the car wasn't tucked away somewhere else, but I figured that Jimmy was a creature of habit and probably had gone home to roost, home being his parents' house.

An older woman answered the door. She was wearing a nightgown and a robe, but it was clear that she'd been up for hours. She invited me in.

"I'm sorry to bother you so early, but is Jimmy Stiles available?"

"Oh, I'll get him," she said with a smile as she turned and yelled, "Jimmmmmyyyy!" Apparently, women at Jimmy's door wasn't unusual.

"What is it, Mom?" I heard him say from the top of the stairs. He clumped down the stairs, then stopped and looked at me expectantly. "Don't I know you?" he asked me.

"Why don't I leave you two young people alone," his mother said as she toddled off to the back of the house, presumably where the kitchen and her morning coffee waited.

An older man came down the stairs, passing Jimmy and me, giving us both a glance. "Hey, Scooter, how's it going?" He ruffled Jimmy's hair. Jimmy tried to defend himself, but it didn't work. His father, I assumed, went the same way as his mother.

"Dad, stop it." Jimmy turned back to me, an abashed look on his face. "Uh, who are you?"

"Mr. Balczeck," I said softly.

He paled, then tried to backpedal. "Uh, if you're selling something, I don't think—" That was Jimmy's idea of getting someone off balance. He pushed me through the door and tried to close it, but my foot was quicker, and so was my hand. I grabbed him by the collar and dragged him outside.

"I'm not selling anything, Jimmy. It's been a few days, but I'm sure you remember who I am, don't you?"

He swallowed hard and nodded. "You weren't there to try to convince Mr. Balczeck that you'd make a good security director, were you?"

"You're catching on. Now I need you to be

straight with me. You know Lisa Browning is dead, don't you?''

He nodded, and his eyes started to blink fast. "Yeah. I know. Home invasion. I still can't believe it.''

"Did you have anything to do with it?''

I'd let go of his shirt by now and he backed up. "Who, me? Why would I rip off my girlfriend and kill her?''

"Not the home invasion, the scam.'' He looked at me like I was a loon. I maintained a stony stare. "That's right. You're the one who gave Lisa the credit card and convinced her to pose as Cynthia MacDonald.''

"What're you talking about?'' He tried to sound indignant, but his tone had a hollow ring. He wasn't putting up much of a fight.

I pressed harder. "Come on, Jimmy, I'm not stupid. Lisa didn't pull off a credit scam all by herself. She probably didn't even know anything about faking someone else's identity and getting stuff free until you showed her how it was done.''

Jimmy had turned sullen by this time. His hands were stuffed in his khakis and his shoulders slumped forward. "It doesn't hurt anybody, it just gets back at the credit-card companies.''

I laughed. "So this is some revolutionary tactic on your part? I don't buy it. By the way, I don't buy the home invasion, either.''

Jimmy's expression transformed from sullen to curious. "What do you mean?''

"By all rights, you're the one who got her killed. She was going to go to the police with what she'd done. I wasn't sure I'd convinced her to give up the names of those in the ring, but she was ready to own up to her part in it." I waited a beat to let it sink in, then said, "You wouldn't happen to know who Spence is, would you? She was talking to me on the phone and mentioned his name."

He looked everywhere but at me. I could see the wheels turning in his head and the panic setting in. "Um, sorry to cut you off, but I have to go."

Jimmy headed for his Miata. I grabbed him again and tried to pull him back. "You have to go to the police with any information you have."

He surprised me by cuffing me upside the head. I staggered back and by the time I'd recovered, he was inside before I had a chance to say anything else. I pounded on the windshield. "Jimmy! Tell me who Spence is and—"

The Miata roared to life and Jimmy peeled out of the driveway.

FIFTEEN

I CALLED ROSA on the cell phone. I knew that she had today off. She answered right away.

"Can you do a job for me?" I hadn't wanted to involve her in this case, but I needed surveillance. I figured Rosa had gotten better at it since being thrown in the pokey the first time.

"Sure, Sarge. What kind of job?"

"Surveillance. Of a guy named Jimmy Stiles. He works at Tech City in Quincy."

"Uh, Sarge? I don't have a car."

"I'll pick you up in fifteen minutes in my Bronco."

I could hear the excitement in her voice. "Cool. I get to drive the Bronco?"

I thought about it. I could probably borrow Raina's Tempo, as long as I got it back to her before she left work. "Yeah, sure."

I called Raina to double-check, then went back and got Rosa. We picked up Raina's car just a few blocks away and Rosa followed me to Quincy. It was raining and cold, typical of Boston weather. When we got to the parking lot, I pointed out the red Miata.

Rosa snorted. "That won't be hard to follow."

"You'll probably spend most of your day in Tech

City. I don't think he's going anywhere. But in case he does—during lunch, or if he gets out early—I want you to follow him. Make notes. And make sure he doesn't see you.''

The first time Rosa did surveillance, she was picked up by the police for loitering outside a jewelry store. The woman she was following got away. I caught the woman on video the next day, jogging around a reservoir even though she claimed to have a bad back.

But this job should be a piece of cake. As a last-minute gesture, I gave Rosa the cell phone and my beeper number, told her to check in with my answering machine every hour, then sent her off to keep an eye on Jimmy.

I was heading back to my office when Bennie the Bond came out of his office, a gun in his hand.

''Matelli!'' he said, looking surprised to see me. He was a small fireplug of a man with a full head of hair, courtesy of the Hair Club for Men.

''Bennie!'' I returned. ''What's up?''

''I was gonna ask you the same thing. I thought you were in your office already. Then I realized you don't wander around in a dark office.''

We both looked down the hall, then at each other. ''You need a gun?'' he asked. ''I can back you up.''

''No, thanks,'' I said quickly. ''I'm sure it's nothing. Probably the cleaning woman. She has a key to the office.''

He didn't look convinced, and I was sure he had his finger ready on nine-one-one by the time I reached my office. The door was closed and the lights were out, both good signs. But when I tried to unlock my door, I locked it instead, a bad sign. I heard rustling coming from inside, something crashed, and just as I unlocked the door, it burst open.

My only impression of the intruder was that he was big. He wore a ski mask and something long-sleeved and dark. Someone forgot to tell him that you wear dark clothes to do your dirty work at night—the office building was half empty on a Saturday, but it was broad daylight outside. I was caught off guard and sent flying backward and down, hitting the marble floor with a thud. By the time I got back up, my intruder had made it to the stairwell and I could hear his footsteps pounding down the steps.

"You all right, Matelli?" Benny was in the doorway, his gun still in his hand. "I called the cops. Someone should be here any minute."

"You didn't happen to get a look at the intruder, did you?"

Benny looked sheepish. "I was on the phone with the police at the time."

I managed to smile. "Thanks, Benny."

"Ah, you're welcome. Hey, if they catch the creep, make sure they give him my number and I'll make bail for him."

"I'll make sure I slip him your card at the line-up."

He laughed and left.

I was torn between running after the guy and seeing what damage had been done in my office. I chose the latter, mostly because I didn't feel like running. I knew it wouldn't do any good. I went inside and winced when I saw the cappuccino machine upended on the floor. The computer was on—someone had tried to access my files, which were all in code. It wouldn't have done them any good. I didn't have any information that they'd want.

I was trying to get the cappuccino machine to work when someone startled me.

"Wow, someone doesn't like you," someone said from the doorway of my office. I looked up from trying to piece together my cappuccino machine. Dana Proux stood there, taking in the destruction. "It wasn't your coffee, was it?"

I managed to laugh at the weak joke. "I make a pretty good cup."

"Hey, why don't I buy you one? There's gotta be a place around here that makes coffee as good as yours."

"I have to wait for the police," I told her.

"I am the police. I intercepted the call at dispatch."

I set the machine back on the small table near the couch and stood up. "Coffee sounds good. I could use something stronger than coffee, though."

I took her to the Moderne Bakery, a wonderful, old-style shop that serves good Italian roast coffee and excellent Italian pastries.

"So what does someone have against you besides

your coffee?'' she asked as we sat with our pastries and coffee.

"I don't know," I said. I closed my eyes. "I found Jimmy this morning."

She perked up. "That's great. He was at his parents' house, right?"

"How'd you know?"

"We were slated to visit them this morning, but were caught up in another homicide."

"He's scared, Dana."

"Scared of what, the police?"

"Well, he ran when I mentioned the police, but I think it was something else, too. It seemed as if he was running *to* something, not just running away. As of this morning, how do the police stand on this case?"

"How do the police stand on the case?" She grimaced. "Standing is the operative word. Nothing's moving. There're no breaks. We've talked to the mother, the ex-husband, the neighbors, and no one knows anything."

"Look," I said, "I've just started to piece a few things together. Lisa Browning did something illegal."

Dana raised her eyebrows in disbelief. I gestured for her not to say anything. "I know, I know. Bear with me." I told her my theory about the true name fraud ring, about how Lisa had gotten involved, and Jimmy's part. I filled her in on my talk with Jimmy today. "He just took off this morning, peeled out of his driveway like he was gonna do something stupid."

"And you have no idea who this Spence is?"

I shook my head. "Clearly the guy in charge of the ring. But I don't know where to start."

"Look, Angie, I appreciate everything you've done. But I don't want to get you in trouble, and I certainly don't want to get in trouble with the department over this case." Dana was avoiding my eyes, looking slightly flushed. "This morning, Sturgeon found the tape and questioned me about it. I tried to cover up, but I'm not a very good liar. He's told me to warn you to stay away from this case because it's still active."

My face must have betrayed my disgust. She patted my hand. "Hey, you've helped keep the file active for maybe a week more than it would have been. Sturgeon hates to have PIs stepping in his territory."

"Yeah, well, I enjoyed the partnership while it lasted," I said, trying not to be bitter about it. The truth was that I liked Dana and was hoping we could be friends. But if I needed help on a case, she wasn't a free operator the way Lee was. She'd have Sturgeon breathing down her back until he retired. "Say, Dana, when is Sturgeon up for retirement?"

We both laughed. Then she looked a little surprised, as if she had just remembered something. "Oh, hey, I stopped by your office to ask if you wanted to get our parents together. What would be a good time?"

We settled for having dinner at my place next week. It would be a surprise.

SIXTEEN

I WENT BACK to my office and cleaned up. Nothing had been permanently damaged, although I wondered if I'd ever enjoy another cup of cappuccino out of my machine.

Rosa checked in with me three times before we got any action. It was a little after noon when I got the call. "Sarge?"

"Yeah, Rosa."

"I'm in your Bronco, and we're heading west. I walked around the store for a while and he seemed nervous and troubled. Later, he came out of the store. He was wearing a different shirt, so I think he's taking the rest of the day off."

"It's possible. Call me when you get to his destination."

A little over half an hour later, I got another call.

"He's stopped at a strip mall in Milton. It looks like he's going into a jewelry store, one of those discount places."

"Rosa, I'm coming down. Where are you and what's the name of the store?"

She described the area. Jimmy was in a store called Facets. I hopped in Raina's Tempo and got there in record time. Jimmy had just left the building. He had a shopping bag in one hand, car keys in the other. I got out of the car and started toward him. He saw me and sprinted for his car. He got there first, locked the doors, and the Miata was out of the parking lot before I had a chance to get back in Raina's car.

Rosa came out of Facets and spotted me. "Sarge! You okay?"

I couldn't contain my disappointment. "I'm fine, but I wish you'd been here to follow him."

She blushed. "Sorry about that. I had to find a bathroom."

I took a deep breath to push down my disappointment.

"It's too bad he spent a few minutes at that house before he came here. I couldn't very well go up to the door and ask to use their bathroom."

I blinked and looked at Rosa. "What house?"

"I can take you there." We got in our respective cars and I followed her. When we got to a large, light blue house set back from the street, she pulled over and stopped.

I got out of the car and went over to her. "What happened here?"

"He got out of the car, went up to the door and rang the bell. A guy answered—young, cute, tall, blond. He was wearing a Celtics shirt. Jimmy stayed at the door while the guy went back in. He came back out with something in a paper bag and handed it to Jimmy. Then Jimmy went to the strip mall and shopped for jewelry."

I thanked Rosa, gave her the keys to Raina's car and took my Bronco back.

"I can stay here, Sarge. You might need someone to back you up."

"Thanks, Rosa, but I think I can handle this myself." I reminded her of Stephanie's birthday dinner at Ma's tonight, and she told me Sophia and Dave would be picking her up. Then I watched her drive away, secure in the knowledge that my little sister would never make a good enough private investigator to ever be in danger.

I walked up to the door and rang the bell. A long fifteen seconds passed before someone opened the door. It was the kid Rosa had described. "Yeah?"

"Hi. I need to talk to you."

His name was Paul Brady and he was a senior at Boston University. He worked at Tech City on weekends for pocket money, and he knew Jimmy a little bit. He wouldn't let me inside, but he stood outside with the door ajar.

"I don't suppose you're one of the decoys who worked the credit-card scam with Jimmy and Spence, are you?"

It would be hard for this kid to lie to anyone. His face turned bright red, for one thing. And he couldn't meet my eyes. "I don't understand. What are you talking about?"

"You're a bad liar, Paul. Just like Jimmy. Why else did Jimmy come over here? You work together."

He smirked. "Hey, he just came to pick something up."

"What?"

"He told me not to tell anyone."

"Paul, do you want to be responsible for Jimmy getting hurt or killed?"

He paused. "No. I don't suppose so."

His response wasn't exactly enthusiastic. "Come on, you could be an accessory to murder. Did you know Lisa Browning?"

His shoulders slumped in defeat. "I lent him my father's gun."

I couldn't believe what I was hearing. This kid went to BU, yet did something stupid like that? "Look, kid, this is important. A woman has already died because of this credit-card scam. Why did Jimmy take the gun?"

"He said it was to protect himself. He said someone was after him."

"Did he say who?"

Paul shook his head. I heard noises in the background like someone else was there.

I was running out of questions. "Where was Jimmy going after he left here?"

"I dunno. Home, I guess."

"Who's Spence?"

The question seemed to throw Paul. "I-I don't know what you're talking about."

A girl came up behind him. She had long, light-brown hair and was wearing those ugly brown-and-green polyester clothes that are in style these days.

She looked at Paul. "That's the name of your boss, Paul, isn't it?"

I hadn't put it together because I only knew Spence's last name: Balczeck. But it made sense. He was a big muck-a-muck with the regional office, but he worked out of a Tech City a few days a week. He was in a perfect position to find the losers like Jimmy and the lost kids, like Paul, who were just thrill-seekers. These were the people who made up his credit-card ring.

While Paul wasn't going to jeopardize his college and the career that would follow by confessing to being part of this ring and fingering Spence, Jimmy was definitely a threat. He had no real future, and he had loved Lisa. When he realized that Balczeck was her killer, he went nuts. Thanks to me and my big mouth. Now Jimmy was going to try to blow away Spence Balczeck.

The only problem was that I couldn't see the scenario going that way. Jimmy was well-meaning, but hardly the type to go up against a ruthless bastard who would beat a young woman to death.

I shuddered as I drove toward Tech City. It was after four, and I knew they closed at five. Traffic had slowed down on 93 South. It was Saturday and people were going home after a day in Boston.

I reached for the cell phone and dialed Tech City.

"Is Spencer Balczeck there?" I asked the youngish voice. I couldn't tell if I was talking to a girl or a guy.

"Um, yeah, he was here. But I think he just left."

"What about Jimmy?"

"He was here asking the same thing, but I haven't seen him for a few hours."

I thanked the person and hung up, feeling somewhat relieved. Maybe Jimmy missed Balczeck and was home, wondering what to do next.

Something had been nagging me all day. I realized it was time to get serious with my client, talk to her about what had really gone on the night before. I called Cynthia MacDonald at home and surprisingly, she answered.

"What do you want?" she asked in a belligerent tone when I identified myself.

"What we all want: the truth." I softened my voice. "Cynthia, it's very important that you tell me what you were really doing on the night Lisa was killed. I've been attacked, my office was broken into, and now a boy is going to go try to kill a man and I'm on my way to stop him. There may be gunplay involved."

There was a long pause, a heavy sigh, and then Cynthia spoke. "I was there that night. I saw a man go into her apartment."

"What did he look like?"

"He was probably fifty, balding, a big man."

"What happened then?"

She sighed in an exasperated manner. "I don't know why I stayed there, watching. I saw the silhouettes on a shade on the second floor, a woman struggling with a man. I heard someone cry out. I just don't know why I stayed. But I did. And I saw him leave. I didn't think he'd seen me, but he must have. He must know who I am from my car license plate or something.'' I could have sworn she was crying. Her voice was shaking. ''I've been getting these calls. No one talks, they just breathe. Not the heavy kind of breathing, just as if they're listening to me, enjoying the sound of fear in my voice.''

The shaking in her voice was getting worse and I suddenly realized that it was the connection. The damn cell phone was wimping out on me. I still hadn't called Dana. I'd planned to. I really had. I shouted into the phone, ''Cynthia, call the police and tell them there's a crime in progress at Tech City in Quincy. Talk to Dana Proux.'' The phone went dead. I was pretty sure she'd heard some of my message, maybe all of it.

It was after five when I got to the Tech City parking lot. The store still had a few lights on, but it was clearly closed.

There was an Americanized Mexican chain restaurant nearby, and I drove over there to use the pay phone. Yeah, cell phones make your life much easier.

Jimmy's Miata wasn't in the Tech City parking lot. I called his house and got his mother.

''No, Jimmy isn't here.''

''Is he working today?''

''He called me just a few minutes ago, dear, and it was terribly hard to hear him, wherever he was. Lots of loud bangs. He said he's taken part of the day off.''

Lots of loud bangs—like guns? "Has he ever expressed any interest in guns?"

Mrs. Stiles was silent for a minute, then said, "Jimmy's never shot a gun in his life. Say, is this a sales call? Are they selling guns over the phone these days?"

"No, Mrs. Stiles—" She'd hung up on me.

I stared at the phone. Guns, a loud place, it might be a shooting range. I checked the phone book. There were three shooting ranges within a few miles of Tech City. I drove to the closest one, and had no luck when I cruised the parking lot. I had better luck at the second range. Jimmy's Miata stuck out like a sore thumb.

When I got to the indoor range, he was squeezing off shots furiously. Anger was coming off him in waves. The smell of cordite hung heavy in the air. I waited until he'd finished a round and was bringing his target forward. He hadn't hit the paper target even once. He stared at it, then at the .38 in his hand, as if he wasn't sure what to do next.

"You're too tense when you fire," I told him.

He turned around quickly, a haunted look on his face. I kept talking. "You need to take a breath and let it out slowly before releasing the trigger. That's the other thing. You don't pull the trigger, you gently release it. It comes easier with practice."

"Why are you telling me all this?" he asked, giving me a suspicious look.

"If you're bound and determined to kill your boss, I can't stop you. I just thought you'd rather see justice done, and get out of jail while you're still young enough to have children. If you kill Spence, you're the one who suffers. He just dies. You stay in jail for the rest of your life.''

"But he killed Lisa, and he didn't show an ounce of remorse.''

"Yeah, that's what sociopaths do, Jimmy. But you're not one and you'll have to live with having killed another human being. Yeah, Spence is the bad guy, but he's still a human being, and the courts still put people away for premeditated murder.''

"I want to kill him. I've spent the last two days acting as if it doesn't bother me. I took the afternoon off to do a job so he'd think I was still in the ring and still thought like him.''

"But you made the detour and borrowed a gun from Paul. How trustworthy is Paul?''

He shrugged. "He's not my best friend or anything like that. But I suppose he's okay.''

"He won't give you up to Spence?''

Jimmy looked uncomfortable. He obviously hadn't thought it through when he went to Paul. "I think he's okay.''

Great, I thought. Paul's okay.

"Look, Jimmy, my best advice, if you decide to take it, is to give me the gun and go to the police.'' I was ready to leave, let him be an idiot. I'd see him in court.

Jimmy looked down at the handgun, back up at me, shifting from foot to foot. "I don't think I can go to the police. Not right now. I want to wait until after Lisa's funeral.''

Okay, I thought. I could understand that. But he was putting himself in danger and I told him so. "The police would probably get you before the funeral. With autopsies backed up, the funeral won't be for another few days."

He started to hand me the gun, then thought better of it. He tucked it in his jacket pocket. "I won't do anything stupid, like run off. I can't be looking over my shoulder for the rest of my life."

"Come on, stop fooling around and give me the gun. You shouldn't even have it anyway. You don't have a license."

He laughed. "I've been part of a credit card ring, the only woman I've ever loved was just killed, and you think I'm worried about firing a gun I don't have a license for?"

I stepped up to him and slapped his face. It threw him enough for him put his hand up to his cheek. "What'd you do that for?"

I held up the gun. "I did it for this."

"Hey! How'd you get my gun?"

"I came in close to you, made you think about something other than the gun, and took it while you were thinking about that other something." I'd learned that trick in the military. It didn't work all the time, but I figured it would work with Jimmy. The subject couldn't be too quick on the uptake and Jimmy fit the bill.

"Call me before you go out there and do something you may regret," I told him, giving him my business card. "You're not a killer, Jimmy."

He looked down. For a man who was thirty years old, he acted like he was still in his early twenties.

"Okay, what do we do?" he asked.

"We call Dana Proux, the homicide detective." I emphasized the "we."

He groaned. "What about the gun?"

I thought about that. "We put it in your car for now, hide it. She has no cause to search your car. She just wants to talk to you."

He didn't look happy, but he finally nodded.

I called Dana from the range office, keeping my eye on a skittish Jimmy. She answered and told me she'd be there as soon as possible. I called Ma in the meantime and told her I'd be late. She gave me grief, but hey, it's my job.

I sat with Jimmy, waiting for Dana to arrive.

"You know this means you can't go back to Tech City, don't you?"

He shrugged. "I can get another job. It didn't pay all that great anyway."

I refrained from mentioning his illegal fringe benefits.

Dana arrived with a squad car.

"I'll call you later," she assured me before taking Jimmy away.

He sat in the squad car, all the fire gone from him, nodding to me like a condemned man before the car drove off. I was relieved that one of my witnesses who could finger Spencer Balczeck was now in protective custody. But I would have felt a whole lot better if I'd kept the gun.

SEVENTEEN

I STOPPED AT HOME and immediately called Cynthia.
I got the answering machine but she picked up when
she heard my voice.

Cynthia was more receptive to my call this time.
"This breather is unnerving," she said. "I have to
screen all my calls now."

"You have caller ID, right?"

"Yeah, but he calls from pay phones. I've already
checked with the phone company."

"Cynthia, you could be in danger. Lisa Browning's killer might be the breather. Get out of there
and head to a hotel for the night. Call Dana Proux
in the morning." I gave her the number.

"I feel safe enough here," she grumbled. "Why
can't I just stay here and not answer the door?"

"This is important, Cynthia, this is your life."

"I can't do this by myself, Angela. Please come
out here."

I felt guilty, but I needed to be at Ma's for Steph's
birthday. I told her that.

Instead of throwing the tantrum I'd expected, she
sighed. "Look, I'll stay in my apartment until you
can get here, how's that? I won't answer the door
or the phone. I live in a secure apartment building."

"I've got a better idea," I said. "Why don't you

stay with a friend or at a hotel? It'd be safer than staying by yourself and waiting for something to happen."

She gave a beleaguered sigh. "Okay, but I really think you're making a big deal out of nothing." Yeah, that's why Lisa Browning was dead. Of course, after Jimmy talked to Homicide about what he knew, Balczeck would be picked up and Cynthia would be safe, as long as she testified against him in court. I gave my client Ma's number and told her to call me when she got to a safe place. She grudgingly promised to do what I asked.

I got out of there after calling Ma to assure her I'd be there, and I'd be hungry. I would feel better when I heard from Cynthia. At least she'd be safe someplace other than her apartment, I thought.

I just hadn't had the time to get my niece a birthday gift. Even Albert had remembered and left something with me to give to Stephanie. I'd have to pick something up on my way to Malden tonight.

I took five minutes to change and wash my face. Things were going along just swell.

I calculated how much time it would take to drive to Malden. I'd probably missed dinner at Ma's, but there were probably leftovers. I'd have to stop somewhere and pick up something for my niece before heading to Ma's. I'd probably be even later, but it was better than showing up without a gift.

I grabbed Albert's bag, which I'd left in the front hallway, and sprinted down the steps to my Bronco. Rosa had told me she'd be getting a ride with Sophia, Dave, and the kids, so I didn't have to knock on her door.

It was after seven-thirty when I got to Malden. I stopped at the only place open on Saturday after five, a drugstore down the road from my destination. The choices were pathetic—painkillers, Maalox, cheap earrings and plastic bracelets, barrettes and Precious Moments figurines. I finally settled on a package of hair clips and a goofy-looking clown troll that held a "Happy Birthday" sign in one plastic hand. I bought a couple of gift bags and a card—I hoped Albert had included a card with his gift, but chances were that if he'd forgotten to wrap the gift, he'd forgotten the card. But I wasn't going to buy a damn card and sign it for him. In the end, I settled for signing his name to my card and putting the gifts together. I drove like a hellion, whatever that was, to get to Ma's before all the food, including the leftovers, was gone.

When I arrived, the faint aroma of Ma's famous sauce, laden with garlic, and pork chops was irresistible from the outside. I raced up the stairs, almost forgetting Stephanie's gifts, and flung open the door. The kids—Ray's, Vinnie's and Sophia's—were in front of the TV, watching some old movie. Vinnie and Ray were sprawled on the sofa. Dave was in an easy chair. The men sported bottles of Heineken, and Vinnie was in the middle of an off-color joke.

Vinnie and Ray looked up at me.

"Hey, Ange," Vinnie greeted me with a salute of his beer bottle.

Ray and Dave both smiled and nodded.

Vinnie looked over his shoulder at the other men. I didn't see it, but I heard it in the intimacy of his tone. "I'll finish that story about the hitchhiker and the priest later."

I put my bags down and crossed my arms. "No, really, Vinnie, please share the joke with all of us, including the women. Hey, maybe Stephanie, Michael, and Ma would be interested in hearing it, too."

"You don't have to be that way, Angie," Vinnie said with a frown. "It was just a funny joke, but not something for the kids or old ladies."

"Funny, all right," I muttered under my breath before answering my brother. "I'm sorry, Vinnie, it's been a tough day and I don't see any regular hours in sight."

Vinnie shrugged.

Ray's eyebrows came together like two caterpillars during a mating ritual. "You must be working way too hard, Angela. The way you're acting, maybe you should think about another profession. Something with regular hours."

I threw my hands up in the air. "The way I'm acting? Do I sound as if I need anything other than a vacation to Mazatlan?"

"Angela Agnes!"

I turned to face Ma, a tiny package of motherhood. She had a dish towel in one hand and both hands on her hips. Her expression was not the pleasant "It's nice to see you," but the "You will not take the Lord's name in vain under this roof" look.

Automatically, I genuflected. "Sorry, Ma. How are you, Ma? You look well."

She seemed to think about it, then smiled. "My bursitis is acting up, but other than that, I'm able to get around."

"Ma, I don't suppose you'd have any food for a starving daughter?"

She raised her eyebrows. "Well, as a matter of fact, we all decided to wait on you. Stephanie seems to like the idea of staying up later."

I took a moment, then a deep breath. She leaned forward and kissed my cheek. "You're a good girl, Angie." She went back to the kitchen. Ma had given up asking me to help around the kitchen for meal-times. I was a pretty good cook, but I didn't work well in groups, causing more chaos than anything else. I usually help with setting the table and clean-ing up afterward. But everything was in place when I looked in the dining room.

I peeked in the kitchen. Sophia was supervising the sauce, and Rosa was bringing the antipasto out of the refrigerator. They both spotted me and waved.

Vinnie's wife, Carla, came out of the kitchen to talk to me. "Angie! What's going on? You look as if you've seen a ghost."

I sighed. "It's been a long day, Carla. How you doin'?"

She grinned. "Vinnie and me, we're gonna have another baby."

I gave her a hug. "That's great, Carla. Congratulations. When are you due?"

"October." Carla was Vinnie's second wife. They already had two kids of their own.

"I'll keep my fingers crossed that it's a girl."

She blushed. "I'll be happy either way, as long as it's healthy."

"Yeah, but a girl would be nice."

Just then, Stephanie came in. Carla looked at her and nodded. "Yeah, a girl would be nice."

"Aunt Angie!" Stephanie gave me a hug.

"Happy birthday, sweetie. Do you feel any older?"

She thought about it. "Yeah. A little. Say, did you know there's a phone call for you? Someone named Dana?"

I gave her a kiss and hustled back into the den, the only place you could have privacy and quiet, which housed Ma's La-Z-Boy, another easy chair, and an end table with a built-in magazine rack. I was relieved that there wasn't a sofa or loveseat in sight. I shut the door and reclined in the La-Z-Boy with the receiver to my ear.

"Look, I've been trying to reach you by cell phone, but I don't get any answer."

"It needs to be recharged," I told her. "Do you want it back?"

"Later. I just thought the cell phone would be a convenience for us to stay in touch about the case."

"So how was Jimmy?"

She laughed. "He didn't deliver."

"What do you mean he didn't deliver?"

"Just what I said. We got him back to the precinct, set him up in a nice interrogation room, and he clammed up."

"So you're leaning on him, right?" I asked, using the lingo Dana was using. I was beginning to feel as if I were in a fifties cop movie.

"He's gone."

"Gone?" I would have played a good parrot in one of those old movies, the way I was repeating the last word every time Dana said anything to me.

"Yeah, we had nothing to hold him on. We brought him back to his car and he took off."

"Well, thanks. You gonna check out this Spencer Balczeck?" I asked.

I could almost hear her shrug over the phone. "I can, if you like. But I have nothing."

"That's not true," I said, and I told her about my client, how she had seen Balczeck coming out of Lisa Browning's apartment two nights ago, how she thought she was safe, but I'd had her check into a hotel and call me when she was really safe. I gave Dana all the information she wanted, except Cynthia's name.

"Come on, Angela, give me a name. How can we protect her if we don't know her name?"

"I need her permission before I release it. I don't think it will be a problem. Just give me an hour. She'll call in. Give me a number where I can reach you."

She gave me her beeper number and we hung up.

I checked my watch. Cynthia should have called me by now. I'd given her Ma's number, but she may have called my office answering machine. I'd have to call and check my machine after dinner. My stomach growled.

From outside the den, I heard the phrase that I love above all others: "Dinner's ready, everybody to the table."

EIGHTEEN

AFTER DINNER, I just wanted to take a nap. But my brothers and Dave were stretched out on all the comfortable chairs, watching a basketball game on the television, and Michael and Vinnie, Jr., were curled up on the floor in front of the set. Stephanie was bugging Sophia.

"When can I open my presents? We've already had dinner. Can I open them now? Pleeease?"

Stephanie's plea took me back to Sophia's birthdays—she had acted the same way, cajoling Ma, climbing on Dad's lap and putting her arms around him, wanting to open her gifts *now*. She had no patience, and neither did her daughter. Of course, Rosa and I *never* acted like that, and the brothers were too cool to show that they cared one way or the other.

Ma came into the living room, her eyes zeroing in on her granddaughter. "Sophia. Let her open her gifts. She's waited so long."

"No, Ma." Sophia crossed her arms. "She has to wait until after we have cake. That's how we always did it when I was growing up."

I noticed Dave had left the living room to help clean up—my dream man. I looked over at Ray, who had fallen asleep in front of the game, his mouth open. He had enough class not to snore or drool, but I bet if something woke him up suddenly, he'd snort. I padded into the dining room to help clear the table. Dave was balancing several plates and bowls.

"You're the child psychologist, Dave," I said. "What do you think about the birthday girl opening her gifts before dessert? Will it scar her forever?"

His raised eyebrows told me that he was not happy at being dragged into this important discussion. No matter which side of the fence he came down on, he couldn't win. If he didn't side with Sophia, he'd never hear the end of it. If he didn't side with Ma, she would manage to bring it up every Sunday for the rest of his life.

Fortunately, Dave is a smart guy. "Why don't you let her open one gift now, have the cake and ice cream, then let her open the rest?"

Stephanie glowed. "Pleeease, Mom? Gramma? Just one gift?"

Sophia relented, Ma seemed satisfied.

"That's why you've got a Ph.D," I murmured, throwing a look of pure admiration in Dave's direction, and he puffed out his chest in mock pride.

When Stephanie was given the okay, she squealed and ran over to the table. After spending a few minutes touching, picking up, and shaking packages, she chose Albert's gift. Ray, Vinnie, and the boys had been rousted from the living room to watch the event before being served cake and ice cream.

"It's a shame Albert had that business meeting

this weekend,'' Ma said as we watched my niece rip into the gift bag and colorful excelsior.

Ray snorted and muttered within my hearing, ''Business meeting, my ass. He works for the mob.''

Ray sensed Ma's sharp gaze upon him and he seemed to shrink into himself. His hands went a little deeper into his pockets, his head bowed, and he honestly looked like a little boy who'd done something wrong. It's amazing how a mother's love can change a person in an instant.

Stephanie squealed again as she pulled Itty Bitty Kitty out of the bag. ''Oooh, she's so cute.'' Stephanie stroked the cat doll's hair.

Michael looked it over nonchalantly and pronounced it ''ooky.''

Stephanie passed it around, getting varying degrees of reactions from my brothers and sisters. It basically ran the gamut from Vinnie and Ray's grunts and puzzled expressions (''Why the hell would anyone want this thing?'' Vinnie muttered under his breath, loud enough for me to hear and kick his shin) to Ma, Sophia, Rosa, and the sisters-in-law fawning over it with coos of delight.

''It's adorable.'' Sophia held it up, stroking the long pink hair and fussing with the moveable arms, legs, and tail. She looked at me. ''Ange, where did Albert get this doll? I didn't see it in any of the stores I visited when I was looking for something for Stephanie's birthday.''

I was at a loss. ''Gee, Sophia, I didn't ask him. I guess I'm not up on the latest dolls these days.''

Ray grunted. "I seem to recall an article about those dolls in one of the small business journals I subscribe to. It's not supposed to be in the stores until June. He must have some connections."

We all fell silent for a moment as we considered what that meant. Carla blinked. "Hey, who's ahead?" She nodded toward the game on the TV.

"Celtics by two," Vinnie replied.

Ma cleared her throat. "Well, I'm sure that Albert has some friends in the toy business. That's probably where he got it."

Carla and Helene glanced at each other, I looked away. Everyone else found something fascinating in the dining room to stare at.

Stephanie's eyes widened. "You mean, I'm the only kid, the first kid, to have Itty Bitty Kitty?"

I winced at the name. Dave smiled. "Yeah, I guess that's what it means."

I got up. "Well, who's for a little cake and ice cream now?"

Carla and Helene, Vinnie and Ray's wives, got up and went into the kitchen. Rosa and Sophia followed.

As I headed for the kitchen, following the other women to supervise placing the candles on the cake, Ma steered me into the den. This was a room that, if it could talk, could recount some very interesting private conversations over the years. Ma used it as a private confessional for her children, their spouses and, no doubt when they've grown to adulthood and have secrets of their own, her grandchildren will be called into the den, one at a time, to tell all.

"What's up, Ma?"

"So Angela, do you know why Albert couldn't come to dinner?" Ma looked a little hurt, but I knew that was just an act. Albert was the one son who didn't bow to her every wish. He was even divorced.

Ma sometimes genuflected over the fact that her youngest son and his wife never had any children. It was bad enough that a good Catholic boy like Albert had to put up with a divorce. But Ma has managed to accept the divorce because Sylvia is an Episcopalian: Since she isn't Catholic, it hadn't been a real marriage in the eyes of the Church, or in Ma's eyes, once Sylvia was out of the picture.

Vinnie has a large family, two kids by his first wife, Bobby and Gina. With Carla, they'd had two kids in four years of marriage, three-year-old Vinnie, Jr., and their one-year-old baby girl, Grace Ellen. Vinnie makes sure that, barring illness, vacation, or more immediate obligations such as weddings and funerals, they come to Sunday dinner.

Ray and Helene have two children. Tommy and Jeff are teenagers and frequently have social commitments on the weekend. But Ray and Helene usually manage to extract their kids from soccer practice or trumpet recitals or theater rehearsal just long enough to see Grandma.

"Look, Ma, you know I don't beat around the bush. We both know Albert has a job that takes him away from family." Okay, I was beating around the bush. It was hard to explain to Ma that he was still with family, only a different kind of family. "What are you really worried about?"

"Have you seen Reginald yet? I hear he stood you up the first time."

I took a deep breath. "He's a doctor, Ma, he gets called in at all sorts of odd hours to the emergency room. We'll get together. Just don't have my wedding planned out before I meet the guy."

Her smile turned coy. "I wouldn't be unhappy about it."

"Ma, it's gonna be a long wait if you're thinking marriage for me."

She bared her teeth, Ma's version of a smile. "I'll keep trying. You know your mother, Angela Agnes."

Yeah, I know her, all right. She'll wear me down until I marry the first guy she approves of. It's gonna be a long battle of the wills. And I'm not sure I'm gonna win.

"Well, this has been nice, Ma, but let's help get the cake ready so Stephanie can blow out her candles. I swear, that kid will explode if she doesn't get to open the rest of those gifts within the half hour."

But she wasn't through with me yet. "A pretty girl like you should have men fighting over her."

"No fights, Ma. Please."

She patted my arm, as if congratulating me on my good fortune—I'd almost had a blind date with a doctor. "Whatever you say, Angela."

Something clicked in my brain. "By the way, Ma, I ran into the daughter of an old friend of yours."

She looked interested. "Oh? Who?"

"Dana Proux. Her father's George Proux. Dana's a homicide detective in South Boston. She's assigned to the murder case I'm working on."

I couldn't believe it. Ma was blushing. "George. I haven't thought of him for years."

"Well, apparently he's been thinking of you a lot lately. Anyway, are you interested in getting together with him for old times' sake?" I couldn't believe I was fixing Ma up with a man. Oh well, she's been fixing me up ever since I turned the age of consent. I didn't mention the little soiree Dana and I had planned for next week—I'd get around to that by tomorrow.

"I'll—think about it and let you know, Angela," Ma said, a pensive look in her eyes. She snapped back to the present. "Now, let's not hold up Stephanie's birthday any more than we already have." Ma went into the kitchen to supervise the lighting of the cake candles.

I hadn't had a serious commitment to one man since I was in the Marines. There had been this one lieutenant in California, Sandy Petrovsky. We had dated for almost six months, and were even talking about moving in together. Then he got a transfer to Korea. He urged me to put in for a transfer as well, but by that time, I was thinking of leaving the service and going back home. I didn't want to be a military wife. Especially if I decided to become a civilian again.

I broke it off gently—long distance. I called and told him I was getting cold feet. I think he was angry with me. I never heard from him again.

Ma left the den and I used those few moments of privacy to make a call to my answering machine. There was no message from Cynthia. I was getting worried. I called her home number and got her machine. I left a message for her to call me, and then went to join the rest of the family.

Everyone was gathered in the dining room, ready to sing "Happy Birthday" to Stephanie, who was enjoying her moment in the limelight with all the dignity of a queen at her coronation.

As the last few words of the birthday song died down, Stephanie glared at us impatiently and said, "Yeah, yeah. Let's get on with it. I want my cake and ice cream now."

Ma cut the cake, I scooped the ice cream and before you knew it, my sweet little niece was opening her gifts. When she had opened the last one, she looked around. "Is that all there is?" I was tempted to tell her that was a song sung by Peggy Lee and was a cynical look at the disappointments of love and life, not about the disappointments of an eleven-year-old girl's birthday party. But I held my tongue.

Sophia finally bent down and said to her daughter, "It's rude to demand gifts, dear. You've gotten plenty."

Stephanie ignored us, grabbed up her Itty Bitty Kitty and began to play. We were dismissed.

I was feeling uncomfortable. Probably just because I wasn't getting any presents. I looked at the time. It was late, ten-thirty, and I decided to check my answering machine. Where was Jimmy tonight? What about Balczeck? And Cynthia, why hadn't she called me?

I stepped into the den to make the call.

Beeep. "Ms. Matelli? Jimmy. You were right about Paul. He told Spence and now Spence is after me. I gave Paul the number where I was at, so I have to move before Spence gets here. I'm really glad I kept that gun." Click.

I closed my eyes. It was all about greed and desperation. I tried to call both numbers for Jimmy, but I woke his parents and they couldn't tell me anything, and his apartment number just rang and rang.

Jimmy'd been smarter than I'd thought he was. He hadn't gotten cold feet at the station, he'd never had any intention of telling the police about the credit card ring and Spence Balczeck. He was planning on killing his boss himself and I'd just delayed the inevitable. He was out to avenge Lisa Browning's death.

Paul Brady had Jimmy's number, and probably knew where Jimmy and Spence were headed for their showdown. I didn't have Paul Brady's number, but I got it from an operator. His line was busy. I'd have to go over there.

I thought about calling the police, but what was I

going to tell them, that some guy might kill his boss because the boss killed his girlfriend? Dana might believe me. I called her precinct number and left a voice-mail message, called her home number and left a message there as well. I remembered her beeper number and called it, but realized I wouldn't be here to take her call. Still, I left the number for her to call me.

It was probably too late to do anything, but I had to try.

I went back to my family to say my farewells. "Uh, Ma, everyone, I gotta go." I turned to Stephanie and gave her a hug and kiss on the cheek. "Hope you had a good one, rugrat. I'll see you later this week." I said good-bye to the other children and to the rest of the family.

Rosa walked me out. I gave her the information and told her to wait until Dana called here. "I'll do my best, Sarge, but I'm at the mercy of Dave and Sophia."

"Your best is all I ask," I said, and kissed her on the forehead.

I wanted to get over to Paul Brady's house as soon as possible, but the only way to get there was through Boston, and at this time on Saturday night traffic was most likely backed up

NINETEEN

WHEN I FINALLY ARRIVED at Paul Brady's house, it was close to eleven-thirty. There was a Jeep there—no red Miata. But Jimmy would be stupid to keep his car here where everyone could see it, especially someone who was out to kill him. I couldn't remember if the Jeep had been here earlier in the day, but I noted there were no lights on in the house.

Before I got out of my Bronco, I got my small flashlight out of the glove compartment. I rang the doorbell and waited a few minutes. No one answered, but I could faintly hear music playing from somewhere inside the house. I tried the door handle, but it was locked. I knocked and waited for another minute, then peeked in a window of the garage and, with the aid of my flashlight, found that one car was there, but another spot was empty. I knew he was probably living with his parents—no college student could afford a place like this.

I followed the music and went around back. I reasoned that someone had to be in the house because no one would leave music on this loud if they were leaving for the weekend or for a late night. The person with the music might be somewhere in the back or in a basement rec room and couldn't hear the doorbell.

The back door was locked, too, but the cellar door was unlocked. I didn't like going into a house without permission, but it was late at night by now, I was starting to get the feeling that something wasn't right. The door at the bottom of the cellar was also unlocked, and I reasoned that this was probably always left that way in case the kids ever locked themselves out of the house.

Once inside the cellar, my rubber soles squeaked on linoleum. It was dark, and my eyes hadn't adjusted by the time something a little heavier than cobweb brushed against my forehead. I tried to wave it away until I figured out that it had a little metal weight attached to the end, and if I pulled the string, light would appear.

The basement indeed had a rec room. At least, half of it was rec room space. I was in the half that was the laundry room. A cheap stereo system, an old couch and two easy chairs, and half of a band's equipment—drums, amps, and bass—were in the rec area. The stereo had been hooked up to the amp so it was twice as loud as necessary.

I climbed the stairs slowly, thinking about calling out. Something stopped me. At the top of the stairs, the door was ajar and I could see part of the kitchen and hear the dishwasher going.

I stepped through, cautious of every step I was taking. I was still working with moonlight and the light of my flashlight. The kitchen smelled of bacon and eggs, French toast, and orange juice from this morning, as well as dishwasher detergent. Dirty designer dishes were stacked next to the sink and the dishwasher made a hissing sound, signaling that it was done with a cycle.

The dining room was next. It hadn't been used recently and seemed more for show and for the occasional dinner party. A lace tablecloth covered the dining table, and a bowl of fresh roses sat in the middle. Against one wall, an antique breakfront held dishes.

A sound, a creak, came from the front part of the house. I finally called out. "Hello, Paul? I'm sorry to barge in like this but—" The front door slammed shut. I made my way to the front of the house, stumbling on a hassock in the living room. By the time I got to the front door, the Jeep's engine was roaring to life and, in a cloud of dust and gravel, took off, fishtailing south toward the highway.

I started out the door when I heard a thump upstairs. For a moment, I wasn't sure whether to follow the car or investigate upstairs. I finally decided to follow my instincts and go upstairs.

I had no gun on me, just my keys stuck between my fingers as a makeshift weapon, the way women in self-defense classes are taught to carry them in darkened parking lots. I followed the sound of someone groaning. In the second bedroom, a boy of nineteen or twenty was lying on the carpet, blood surrounding him. He'd been beaten in a similar way to Lisa—at least from what Dana Proux had described to me.

I knelt beside him and saw he was still breathing,

but with difficulty. I quickly searched and found a phone and, using a handkerchief I carry for such purposes, picked up the receiver and dialed nine-one-one. While I was waiting, I felt for a pulse. It was faint, and getting fainter.

"Emergency." The voice sounded like it had heard it all. It should have had a calming effect on me, but I became more agitated.

"Get an ambulance out to fourteen-eleven Weston Drive immediately. A young man has been severely beaten and I'm not sure he's going to make it."

"Name?"

"Paul Brady."

"No, *your* name, ma'am. The ambulance is on its way already."

"What the hell difference does it make?"

I gave her my name. Just as I hung up, I heard the front door open and close. The ambulance couldn't be here already. I hadn't heard it. Besides, the front door was locked. It could be Paul's attacker, but why would he come back?

"Paul?" The voice was thin and young. Light footsteps ran up the stairs. "I've been waiting for you out front for five minutes. You wanted to go to the—" She stopped in the doorway when she saw me, then him. The intake of breath, the whiteness of her face, the way she swayed told me that she wouldn't stay on her feet for long. I got up and took a step toward her.

She took a step back. "Stay away from me. I'm going to call the police."

"I already did," I replied. The sound of sirens backed me up. She visibly relaxed a bit. She was pretty, fresh-faced, thin, and about seventeen years old. Her pale brown hair was long and wavy. I remembered she was the girl who had been here with Paul earlier today. I looked back at Paul, then at her. "Do you know anything about this?"

Her eyes widened and she hesitated a fraction of a second too long. "I don't know what you mean."

"Lisa Browning was murdered the other night. She was involved in a credit scam ring."

The girl looked back at her boyfriend, lying on the floor. He wasn't groaning anymore. The sirens had stopped and someone called out, "Paramedic."

"Up here," I said loudly. I heard their footsteps on the stairs and a moment later, a thirtyish-looking man in uniform, carrying a red metal box, had entered the room.

I stepped out of his way and turned on some lights, taking the girl by the arm and guiding her out of the room.

"What's your name?" I asked as we headed down the hall.

She couldn't look at me. "Bonnie. Bonnie Lightfeather."

I wondered about her last name—it sounded almost made up, but she might be part Native American.

"Well, Bonnie, my name is Angela Matelli, and I'm a private investigator."

She looked up, fear in her eyes. "You're the one Paul and Jimmy were talking about. The PI." I could hear the walkie talkies squawking, and a few moments later, another paramedic came up the stairs, carrying some equipment.

"Excuse me, ma'am?" a paramedic called. Several other medics were congregated in the hall. A stretcher was being wheeled up the stairs.

"Yes?" I replied.

"This boy needs to go to the hospital. How can we contact his family?"

Well, duh, I thought. Blood all over the damn carpet and this yoyo tells me Paul needs medical attention? I turned to Bonnie, who was crying now, her face streaked red with tears. "Where are his parents, Bonnie? How can they be reached?"

"They—they went to the Cape today. To their beach house." She was sobbing now, and I could barely understand her.

"Where? Do you have the number?" I grabbed her shoulders, shaking her a little to get her to calm down. Not that I was being much of a help.

She got herself together enough to be led by a young, muscular paramedic downstairs to contact Paul's parents in freakin' Wellfleet or wherever. Meanwhile, pandemonium was happening on the stairs. The paramedics were bringing Paul's inert form down the stairs and working on him the whole way. It didn't look good.

The paramedic who had been first in Paul's bedroom came over to me. "He's probably not going to make it. The police are on their way."

He didn't say it to me, but the implication was clear—I was not to leave the scene of the crime before the police arrived. The problem was that I had a feeling there wasn't much time before the murderer covered his tracks. Jimmy was after Balczeck and I had no doubt who'd win out, despite Jimmy's good, but misguided, intentions. If he'd talked to Dana like I'd asked him to, he wouldn't be about to face a ruthless killer.

I wandered downstairs and found the girl, Bonnie, sitting on the living room couch, hugging herself and rocking back and forth.

I approached her, but she didn't seem to notice me until I was sitting across from her.

"Bonnie," I said gently, "I think it's time for you to tell me everything you know."

She gave me a petulant look. "You brought this all down on us. You're responsible for what happened to Paul. And Lisa. We were just doing it for fun, and for some extra money. It didn't hurt anyone."

I refused to get caught up in a game of "who's guilty," so I went on as if she hadn't said it. "Spencer Balczeck killed Lisa and Paul. He's covering his tracks. Jimmy is next, and you're probably on the list, too."

She looked at me, big, shiny tears in the corners of her eyes started to drop. "Spence has a room at

Tech City where he stores the stuff he's going to fence. No one suspects a thing because he's a big wig at the regional office and has taken over the Quincy Tech City for his own uses.''

It made sense to me—the warehouse was full of electronic equipment. No one would suspect it was being used to harbor the merchandise from the credit card scams. Who would notice another television or computer? As far as jewelry went, it was so small, Spencer probably kept it in the safe in his office.

She touched my arm. ''I'm sorry I tried to blame you for their deaths. I know it wasn't you. Spencer kept telling us we weren't hurting anyone and the money was so good—''

I patted her arm in sympathy, then went to look for a phone that wasn't in the general crime scene area. I found a bedroom upstairs that that been closed off, and it looked like it was Paul's parents' bedroom. The crime scene hadn't touched this room.

I tried to call Dana Proux again. I was in luck, she was at home. Briefly, I told her what had just happened and what Bonnie had just told me.

''I have some news for you, too,'' Dana told me. ''Sturgeon is interviewing Cynthia MacDonald at Mass General. She was beaten up a few hours ago— she gave us your name, says she should have followed your advice. She escaped before he killed her, but she gave us information about Spencer Balczeck. Don't do anything stupid, Angela, this guy is an ex-Green Beret and has a history of violence.''

"Jimmy Stiles is after him. He left a message on my machine."

The detectives had arrived and were looking around. I asked Dana to stay on the phone for a few minutes. The detective who approached me wasn't impressed that I was a private investigator, but that changed after I put him on the phone with Sergeant Proux from the South Boston precinct to fill him in.

There were a lot of "Uh-huhs" from the detective on my end, the occasional glance at me as if he was making sure I matched some description that Dana was giving him.

"Okay, Sergeant. I hope you don't mind if I confirm it with someone higher up the food chain." He listened a minute. "Uh-huh. Thank you Sergeant." He turned to one of his officers. "Go out to the car and check on a Sergeant Dana Proux at the South Boston station. I wanna know if she exists and if she's legit."

When he finally handed the phone back to me, he said, "That was convenient, having a detective on the line to vouch for you. And I'm not crazy about you using a phone on the scene of the crime."

"Oh, come on, detective," I replied, "I'm not a chimp. I used the phone in the parents' bedroom. The door was closed when I came on the scene, and there was no sign of the crime having been committed, even partially, in here."

"Don't you have a cell phone like most of the twentieth century these days?" he asked, annoyed that I was right.

"It needs to be charged," I replied. So much for the twentieth century. And I didn't even want to admit that it was a borrowed cell phone.

He took out his notebook and pen, then got all the vital statistics from me. I gave him a description of the scene when I arrived, except I didn't mention that I'd come in through the back door.

When I finished my explanation of the last few days' events, he consulted his notebook. "So you're saying you didn't see the perpetrator here, but you got a look at his vehicle."

"Yes. It was a black or dark blue Jeep Grand Cherokee. Probably 1996."

A uniformed cop came into the room. "Lieutenant? We're ready for you."

He turned his back to me. "Excuse me."

"No problem," I said to his back. "I'll just hang out here."

Bonnie hugged herself. "I liked Lisa, but she was bothered by what we were doing."

"And you weren't?" I watched the expression of the young girl in front of me. She was pretty, came from a good family, had everything going for her. She probably got good grades at school and would attend an Ivy League college when she graduated high school.

She pulled her long hair back from her face, running her fingers through a section of it. She looked straight at me, the naïveté shining in her eyes. "It didn't bother me much. I figured most of the people whose identities were used wouldn't have to pay for it. They'd just have to report that someone else was using their credit and by then, we'd be on to another identity. We always go into large discount-type stores to get instant credit. No one remembers us a couple of days or a week or a month later.''

"You really believe it didn't hurt anyone? It's called true name fraud, and it ruins people's lives,'' I said. She looked as if she didn't believe me. She was young, had never had to work for a living, never had to build up her credit. I thought about explaining it to her, but I had a feeling I'd be wasting my time. I could only hope that her parents would care enough to let her go through the system and see what happens when you break the law.

"Why would kids like Paul or yourself, obviously from a stable, wealthy background, do something stupid like this? Call your parents and have them retain a lawyer.''

She looked as if it was hitting her for the first time. Her expression turned bleak. "We were bored. It was exciting. When we first started going out a few months ago, Paul told me that he'd met a guy who had a cool Miata. He wanted one like it, but he knew his parents wouldn't get it for him. Jimmy told him he knew a way of making enough money to buy it himself. Paul jumped at the opportunity. When he came back from his first run, which was out in Mattapan, he was pumped. He told me what a rush it was to pose as someone else, get credit, and buy up to the limit.''

"So all of this happened because Paul just wanted a really cool car,'' I said. Now Paul was dead. It didn't look like he would ever get that really cool car.

A uniformed cop came into the living room. "Ma'am?" I blinked, looking around to make sure he was talking to me. "You can leave. We checked out your police contact. The lieutenant has your address and phone number. Stop by the station tomorrow. He'll want you to make a formal statement."

"Uh, thanks," I replied. "Listen, Lieutenant, I'm going to Tech City in Quincy right now."

He looked at his watch. "I think they close at eleven. It's one in the morning right now."

"No, no, I'm going there because I think this young man's killer is going to destroy all the evidence that could be used against him in the true name fraud ring. Would you do me a favor and call the Quincy police and have them meet me there?"

He gave me a strange look. "I thought all you PIs were cowboys, wanted to do things your way."

I held up my hands. "Not me, buddy. I just want to see a killer brought to justice. I just figured you'd pull more weight with the Quincy police than I would."

He nodded. "Okay. I'll do it. It'll take you about half an hour to get there. I'll let them know."

I thanked him, then glanced at Bonnie. She was crying again. Only I wasn't sure if it was for Paul this time.

"If I were you," I told her gently, "I'd tell that detective over there everything you told me. And get a good lawyer, kid."

I left, this time using the front door.

TWENTY

I DROVE AS FAST as I could. This time, traffic was fairly light. Of course, it was one in the morning. I had tried dialing the Tech City number while I was at the Brady residence, but I got a recording telling me that the store closed at eleven. I don't know why I thought Spence, the killer, would answer the phone. I wondered if the police were there already.

I screeched into the parking lot at one-twenty. I could see the Miata in the parking lot, but no Jeep. I knew Balczeck had to be here. When I got to the door, the lights were being turned out.

I wished I had use of the cell phone again to call the police and let them know that the Jeep was here, but all I got was static.

I did the next best thing—I tried to open the door by force. Yeah, that worked. The door rattled and probably alerted Balczeck that I was there. Alone. Great.

There had to be a way to get in because Balczeck had to be getting rid of the evidence against him. I wondered about Jimmy, if he was still alive. I started to creep around the side of the building. There was a loading dock in back and it was my best way to get in. When I got around to the back, sure enough, the Jeep was parked there, and so was a large moving van. I wondered how much stuff Balczeck had in that warehouse. Slipping around and under the van's ramp that rested against the loading dock, I could hear movement from inside the warehouse. Someone's heavy footsteps came up the ramp and went into the van.

I seized the opportunity to peek out and noticed that there wasn't anyone else around. I slithered up and rolled into the warehouse behind some boxes. From my floor vantage point, I could see the boots of the person as he walked back into the warehouse and picked up more boxes. When he moved back into the van, I got up and moved farther into the warehouse and toward where I was guessing was the store's location.

I stumbled over some boxes—big surprise—and froze. I didn't hear anything out of the ordinary, no running boots, no shots in the dark, no one yelling for me to come out. Maybe he hadn't heard me. In fact, I heard him starting up a forklift and I started to head toward the back of the warehouse, the front of the store, again.

I suddenly realized the forklift sounded like it was coming closer to me instead of toward the ramp area. I looked around and heard the hit before I saw it—a pile of boxed TVs fell over toward me. I jumped out of the way and heard a man laugh.

"Hey, that must be Angela I almost got."

I started to run. A beam of light in the darkened warehouse was suddenly following my every movement and I realized the forklift was behind me. A wall of boxed CD players suddenly loomed up ahead of me and I swerved to the right just before I ran into them. I heard the forklift slam into them and someone swore. I felt along the wall until I came to a door. It wouldn't give at first. I tugged harder, then suddenly, I was in a hallway.

Where the hell were the cops? I could imagine them swarming into the parking lot, finding Jimmy's Miata, my Bronco, and not finding anyone else. What would they do?

I tried the first door on the right, but it wouldn't budge. I kept going, trying the second door, then the third, which finally gave. I stumbled into a dark room just as I heard Balczeck come through the door from the warehouse.

"Angela, I'm gonna find you. You can't escape," Balczeck called out.

I suppressed a shudder. Yeah, he'd find me, but not before I called the police. I'd locked the door, which, if he had keys, would last a few precious moments as I fumbled for my flashlight. I swept the light around the room carefully, looking for a phone. When I located it on a desk in a corner, I called nine-one-one. Voice mail came on, but I put it on hold and kept it there. The police would record the call, the place it came from, and investigate. I saw the phone light go out and heard a laugh.

"Calling the police won't do you any good, Angela," Balczeck called out again. "I can hang up on any call you try to make out of here."

I was getting tired of this. He meant to frighten

me, and I had to admit I was scared, but what Balczeck didn't know about me was that when I got scared, I got mad, too. I didn't answer him, didn't want him to have the satisfaction of hearing my shaky voice.

I took stock of the room. It had a computer desk, a phone, a file cabinet, two tables against two separate walls, and computers on both the desk and on one of the tables. The light switch was in an unusual place—you had to walk in the room and around the door to get to it.

There was also a bunch of computer cable and duct tape lying on the floor near the computer on the table, obviously from a recent installation. I could hear Balczeck checking the second room. He'd be here soon. I took the duct tape and taped up the light switch with several swatches of the stuff—I continued the duct tape for a while along the wall, making it difficult to tell in the dark where it began and where it ended. It would be easier not to turn on the light than to try to take the tape off.

I grabbed the cable and started winding it, about calf-high, around the desk legs and the table legs, stretching the cable across the open spaces where a person would walk. I'd have to memorize where I'd put it so I could avoid those areas. After I'd quickly secured the cable, I searched the desk, and found a steel letter opener. I heard a key rattling in the door, the knob turned and I shut off my flashlight, standing in a place where he wouldn't see me right away.

The door opened and he stepped inside. There

was a faint light from the hallway—he apparently had wanted to shed some light on this situation. I heard him swear when he couldn't figure out what was wrong with the light switch. I made a noise deliberately and he turned my way. I shined my light on his eyes.

"Don't make this more difficult than it has to be, Angela," he said as he moved toward me. I saw the gun in his hand and he pointed it in my direction and fired. But I ducked, and he tripped over my makeshift tripwire and went down. I leapt nimbly over a part of the cable and got out of there, closing the door behind me to slow him down.

Geez, where were the cops? I thought as I headed down the long hallway. It had to end, and soon, it did. And just in time. Balczeck had recovered and was stumbling out of the office. He fired in my direction again and I felt a bullet graze my leg as I dove through the doors that led to the store.

I dragged my carcass toward the CD section and hid in the Alternative music section. This was one time I wished I had my gun. But no, I had to leave it behind in my office, like it was doing me any good in there. Any more good than my aikido skills would do me in a confrontation with Balczeck and his gun.

I looked around, crawling on my hands and knees, hoping Balczeck wouldn't go to the trouble of turning on the lights. Or maybe he should—lights in a store at this hour would certainly bring the police. And that was why he tried to find me in the dark— an advantage for me, and one I tried to use.

I needed to find Jimmy. I didn't think he was out here on the floor. He might be in his car, already conveniently dead. I tried to think like Balczeck. He preferred other people to do his work for him, so he probably had Jimmy tied up somewhere and wanted to move the body while Jimmy was still alive—then he'd kill him.

I had to check the other offices I passed on my way back there. I'd have to distract Balczeck. I grabbed a CD and threw it toward the front. Not only did Balczeck go in that direction, but he fired a shot and shattered a display window. A no-no if you're trying to kill someone without drawing attention to yourself. I didn't think Balczeck would have a job with Tech City tomorrow, if he was able to come to work at all.

I slipped out of the store and into the hallway again, keeping low so Balczeck wouldn't figure out I'd left. I tried the doors, and Balczeck had left every door he'd tried, unlocked. Sure enough, Jimmy was tied up and a little worse for the wear in Balczeck's own office.

I took a pocket knife I always carry and slit the duct tape around his ankles and wrists. Then I ripped the tape off his mouth. He winced but stayed silent. I was hoping we could get out of there through the back door, but after helping Jimmy to stand and walking out into the hallway, I noticed that the forklift was blocking the warehouse door. Balczeck was definitely ex-military—he'd thought of everything.

We started toward the front again, and Jimmy let me go out first, being the gentleman he was.

A hand grabbed my arm and roughly turned me around. I still had the knife out, so I relaxed into Balczeck's grip. Then I turned toward him and the knife connected with his shoulder. Spence grunted and dropped his grip. I danced away.

He recovered, looked up at me and smiled. Not a nice smile, now that I thought about it. "Hey, Angela. Glad to see you here."

Slowly, I backed away.

"You know it's over, don't you, Angela?"

"No, I know no such thing. Stay away from me."

"What? You're gonna call the cops?" Balczeck laughed. "That's what Jimmy was gonna do. He got cold feet when he realized that Lisa had been murdered. I tried to talk some sense into him—Jimmy loved her, but he made a mistake by bringing her into the ring. I could tell she had too much of a conscience. And I had to take care of that mistake."

"But it's escalated into more than one mistake, hasn't it?" I asked. I wanted to keep him talking. That's what you're supposed to do, right?

He shrugged. "A few." He wasn't much of a talker.

But I made up for it. I smiled. "In fact, you have more to deal with than you realize. You left Paul for dead, but he's still hanging in there." No use letting him think he got away with something. "And his girlfriend? She saw Paul's condition and she's singing like the fat lady at the opera. You're going to jail, bub. Killing Jimmy and me won't help you.''

He shrugged, not seeming all that concerned. ''I can still get out of the country. I've got my passport and some spending money here in my office safe. And there's a few nice pieces of jewelry I can sell when I'm gone.''

''So you don't need to kill us. You can just go.''

He smiled and shook his head. ''Sorry. Gotta cover my tracks.''

I acted as if he wasn't unnerving me. My insides were jelly. ''How long have you had this operation?''

''Three years. And it's been very successful. I have a network out there that's unbelievable.'' He looked at me appraisingly. ''I like you, Angela. I don't want to hurt you. Why don't you join me? I could use a woman with your resourcefulness.''

''Uh, yeah, sure,'' I said. ''Sounds fascinating. And I bet the benefits are terrific. When do I start?'' I started to look around for any sign of life. Where was Jimmy? He probably found a way around that forklift. Maybe he was going for the cops. Maybe he was just going. Where the hell were the cops?

Balczeck smiled. ''I bet you're wondering where the cops are.''

I tried to look nonchalant.

''This is the new location for this Tech City. Cops probably don't even know where this one is.''

''I wouldn't bet on it. Quite a few of them probably have shopped here.''

The place was still completely dead, like I would be if I didn't think of something fast.

Balczeck shook his head with a regretful smile. "I wish I could believe you, Angela. About wanting to join me, I mean. I really do. But I know you'd say anything. And the first thing you'd do is go to your police friends." He was gonna pull the trigger. So much for my aikido skills. I was definitely not faster than a speeding bullet.

He gestured toward the door, wanting me to go back out to the office where he'd bind me with duct tape, beat me senseless and kill me. No way, I thought. I feinted like I was going through, but I dove to the side instead.

There was no time to look back. A running target would be hard for him to shoot. At least, that was the theory. He fired at me anyway and I felt the heat of a bullet graze my arm. I stumbled, but kept going. Balczeck was out of shape, so I was able to get a good head start. My only chance of getting out of this alive was to find a place where there was a phone and a locked room, but that was back in the hallway, and that was a deathtrap. I hid in the television aisle, keeping low. When I got to Aisle 3, I saw movement in Section B. Jimmy had found his way out here without Balczeck finding him.

"We have to keep moving," I whispered.

He was breathing fast. I saw a movement behind him, so I pushed Jimmy aside and rolled the other way. A bullet hissed between us.

"I don't think either of you will be going anywhere,'' Balczeck called out. "I'm sorry, Jimmy, but I can't let you leave now. You know too much.''

That last line almost made me laugh, it was so melodramatic. Then I reminded myself that he'd killed two people and was aiming for three and four. Bonnie Lightfeather might be the only one to get out of this alive, and if Spence got away and she testified against him, she'd be looking over her shoulder for the rest of her life.

"Angela, where are you? Let's get this over with.''

"The hell we will,'' I muttered. I held my breath. And stayed very still. Jimmy followed my example. My first priority was to get this witness out of the building before Spence used us for target practice. He was nearby. I could feel his presence.

Hiding in the dark reminded me of maneuvers in the service. I looked around for a weapon, anything. Of course, I didn't tote my gun around, and I'd noticed that the only time I ever needed it was when I didn't have it.

I'd thought it out earlier as to why Balczeck didn't turn on the lights, and I thought maybe we should do it. Then I realized that if we did, people might think Tech City was open and come to the doors. Then Balczeck would have to kill a lot more people.

That gave me an idea. This would be the moment in a movie where the heroine sneezes. Fortunately, I didn't. But Jimmy did. Actually, he whimpered.

Nothing bad happened. I let out the breath I'd been holding. Too soon, apparently.

A beam of light swept the store, coming close to where we were bunkered. I grabbed Jimmy and we ran in a crouched position until we were in the computer section.

"Let's move toward the back," I said in a low voice.

He nodded.

"Let's go," I said, pushing him toward the back of the store. The flashlight beam swept over us and Spence got another shot off, this time hitting me in the arm.

I yelped, not an encouraging response from a tough lady PI.

"Are you okay?" Jimmy asked.

"I'll live." I inspected the damage. A bullet had passed through the fatty part of my upper arm. It was a clean wound, entry and exit, so Balczeck wasn't using those exploding bullets that do lots of damage. I guess he was an old-fashioned guy—give the quarry a fighting chance. And I was going to fight.

We needed to get moving now. Jimmy helped me get to the back of the store, the warehouse.

"The door is right back there. We can both make it," he said.

I could hear Spence moving around in the front of the warehouse. He was knocking boxes around, yelling for me and Jimmy. It was time to move. As

I headed down an aisle, I spotted a push broom, just the thing.

I was pretty good with the *jo,* or staff, in aikido. I didn't have to try to break the brush off over my knee—it just unscrewed. I hefted the handle a few times, tried a few moves, then moved along the wall to the door. My arm hurt, but my life was at stake.

Spence was nowhere in sight. I stepped out into an aisle, still staying as silent as possible. The aisle was empty.

I crept down to the next aisle. Spence's back was to me, and he was walking carefully. He didn't look so sure of himself anymore. I slipped out of my shelter and crossed the aisle quietly.

It was at that moment that another shot was fired. But it didn't come from Spence. It was Jimmy. The moron was trying to get another shot at Balczeck, and I could have been killed. I was pissed. He'd probably stayed behind in the office to get the gun that Balczeck had taken away from him, and he'd had it the entire time we were making like commandos in the store. If we got out of this, I was going to kill him.

Balczeck looked up and caught sight of Jimmy. He pointed his gun, and Jimmy just stood there like a deer in headlights. This was the reason Jimmy had waited so long to fire a shot. He needed to be close to Balczeck, and even then, he'd blown it.

I moved as fast as I could on one and a half pins. Spence heard me coming—a lovestruck bull moose in a china shop was probably quieter—but he didn't turn around quickly enough. I whacked his gun hand and heard the gun clatter to the ground.

With his free hand, he grabbed the end of my *jo,* which was just fine with me. I was ready for that and went with it. The nice thing about aikido is that it's all self-defense. You can't really attack anyone with it, but you can defend yourself by using your attacker's force against them. So when Spence tried to pull it out of my grasp, I surprised him by stepping into the movement and twisting his wrist. It caught him off balance and he grunted with pain when I got his wrist in *nikkyo,* a submission hold that made it impossible for the attacker to let go, and kept him on his knees.

Stepping behind him and turning, he had no choice but to follow my lead. With another twist, I had Spence on the ground, the *jo* across his neck and shoulders.

"Agh! Let me up, bitch."

"Now, now. That's no way to talk to the woman who's holding a staff against your neck." I put my weight against the *jo* and he grunted again. "I might get careless and press down a little too much, snapping your neck in two."

Jimmy turned the lights on and limped over to us just as cop cars pulled into the parking lot. They were moving kind of slow, but they had their flashing lights on, which was nice of them.

When Jimmy got closer, I noticed the marks on his wrists where the duct tape had been wound tight, and bruises were starting to form all over his face and arms. He had his gun in one hand and he was pointing it at Spence.

"Don't be a putz, Jimmy," I said, "let the police sort this one out. Go out front and let them in. You're damn lucky I'm busy at the moment because if the cops don't put you in the squad car, I'll put you in the hospital for pulling a stunt like that with the gun."

Jimmy shrugged and moved toward the shattered window.

TWENTY-ONE

AFTER THE POLICE TOOK Spencer Balczeck away, Dana Proux arrived on the scene. I had requested that she be here, and the Quincy police had obliged. She had dressed hastily—I'd obviously gotten her out of bed.

"Look at you, girl," she said to me, "you're a mess. You need to go to a hospital and have them take a look at that wound of yours. Want me to call an ambulance?"

Now that she mentioned it, the wound was starting to sting. I felt a little pale, but I was still on my legs.

"Nah. I can drive myself to the hospital." I started to walk, but I was shaky.

Dana came up to me. "Look, where is your car? It shouldn't be sitting here in Quincy anyway. Why don't I drive you? One of the officers can take my car back to the station."

I hadn't really wanted to drive myself, but I didn't want to get in an ambulance after watching the body of Paul Brady being taken away by one. And I definitely wanted to go to one of the hospitals in Boston proper, not one of the hospitals out here in the boonies. One of the paramedics examined me and told

Dana that I was okay for a ride to a Boston hospital.
Dana gave the keys to her car to one of the uniforms.

We ended up at Mass General's emergency entrance. It was the closest hospital that was on my
HMO plan. It was actually a quiet night in the emergency room. There were people milling around, but
most of them were quiet. No red ambulance lights
flashing, no shouts of "Stat! Stat!" coming from the
entrance. I guess I'd been watching too many of
those medical dramas lately. That was a clue that
my love life wasn't exactly heating up. I couldn't
say the same about my professional life.

"Your client is staying here, Angela. You should
look in on her," Dana told me. "Of course, it's three
in the morning—" She grinned. I managed a grin
and a thanks in return. "By the way, you don't have
to come in to give me your statement until later
tomorrow."

"Oh, thanks," I replied as sarcastically as I could
manage. "I only have to give statements to the
Braintree and Quincy police."

"Try to fit me into your busy schedule," she said
in a dry tone.

A police car picked up Dana to take her back to
the South Boston precinct—but not before I asked
her for one more favor—to call Rosa for me and tell
her where I was.

After less than half an hour, I was wheeled into
a cubicle. The nurse took my blood pressure and
temperature, then she left. The doctor came in a few
minutes later, obviously harassed. He was good-

looking, dark, curly hair, wire-rim glasses perched on a straight Roman nose. He had a very dark five o'clock shadow, which told me he'd been up all night, probably pulling double shifts.

His tag read "R. Giordano, Resident M.D." Giordano—the name sounded familiar, but I was in such pain by now that I didn't focus on it. He read my chart. "Ms. Matelli?" He looked at me over his wire rims and smiled. "Reginald Giordano. Most of my friends call me Reg." He held out his hand.

Puzzled, I was shaking his hand when it hit me. This was my blind date.

"I'm glad to have a chance to meet you finally," he said. "I hope you didn't think I was trying to get out of it."

I wasn't in much of a mood for conversation, and he was a good enough doctor to figure that out for himself. It was probably my dazed look. He went professional on me and took a look at the wound, cleaned it out, gave me a tetanus shot, wrapped it, and gave me something for the pain.

When he was done, he smiled. "Look, my shift ends in a couple of hours. You're definitely ambulatory, but I think I can find you a bed in the doctor's lounge for the time being. Think you'll stick around and go out for that dinner we never had? Of course, it would be breakfast."

It had been a hell of a couple of days. Now, all of a sudden, I had a date.

In the meantime, I figured I'd be hungry in a couple of hours, and a bed sounded really good. Sleep sounded really good. And breakfast with a handsome doctor wasn't the worst way to end a shift.

"That sounds like a date to me, Doctor," I said. I tried to keep my eyes open. "Hey, I gotta call my little sis, tell her not to worry about me." I was getting fuzzy around the edges.

Reg took care of it for me—he got the number from me just before I drifted off.

TWENTY-TWO

SEVERAL DAYS LATER, Cynthia walked back into my office. She wasn't as humble as I'd hoped—not following my advice had almost gotten her killed. Spence had put the doorman out of commission and gotten his set of keys out of the office. Cynthia was asleep when he let himself into the apartment, and it was only a whim that kept my client from being killed. She'd stacked pots and pans next to the door so they were knocked over when he tried to enter. She managed to dial nine-one-one and hide the phone before he got to her, but things could have gotten a lot uglier if she hadn't been a quick thinker.

All in all, I think Cynthia MacDonald would agree that a hotel room would have been a lot cheaper and the room service would have been a hell of a lot better than nurses sticking needles everywhere and making you wear humiliating gowns that show your goose pimply backside to the world.

Now she was out and the bruises were still there but she'd covered them up with lots of makeup. And she was writing a check to me for the work I'd done to clear her name.

"Of course, your name isn't magically cleared, you know," I told her.

"There's a lot of paperwork to fill out," she replied. "I've retained my lawyer to handle the details."

Wow—she thought these were going to be details. Boy, was she in for a surprise. She'd have credit problems for years to come. But who was I to spoil her delusion, I thought as I took the check, smiled, and accepted her thanks.

I'd checked in on Mrs. O'Connell to see how Jessica was doing. She told me that her granddaughter was sad, but that she was going to a therapist, courtesy of her father, and he had promised to turn over two thirds of the money he would be getting from the insurance policy. It was a nice thought. I hoped he followed through with it. Money could do strange things to people when they got their hands on it. It was nice to promise others a share in your good fortune, it was another thing to follow through on it. I hoped Tim Browning kept this promise to his daughter.

As for Ma and George Proux, the dinner went well the other night. Dana and I set it up, Dana and her dad going to dinner at a restaurant, Ma and me just "happening" to meet them there. At first, George seemed more delighted than Ma, but she warmed up as time went on, and pretty soon they were cozying up to each other and ignoring us kids in the corner. I felt like tiptoeing out of there, but Dana and I just went over to the lounge area and had a few drinks.

I guess Ma and George are planning to see each other again next week. I think she was concerned about the fact that she wasn't properly divorced, but she seems to have gotten over the fact that she's stuck with our father until one of them dies. And George just loves to be with her. I don't know what the future has in store for them, but they're happy right now.

As for Reg, we had our breakfast at Max's Deli Cafe, found we had a lot in common—wonderful but overbearing mothers and absent fathers, a similar taste in music and books, and he likes iguanas. I promised to take him home to meet Fredd, my watch iguana.

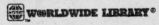

AN ELLIE BERNSTEIN/LT. PETER MILLER MYSTERY

Beat Up A Cookie

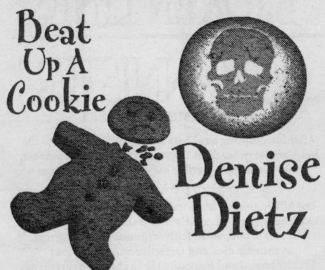

Denise Dietz

Ellie Bernstein is still a fan of the TV series *M*A*S*H**. So are a lot of other people in Colorado Springs. In fact, years ago they gathered to watch the show's finale, and everyone came as their favorite character.

Now, after having lost fifty-five pounds at Weight Winners, Ellie sure looks a lot more like Hot Lips, but that claim to fame might be dangerous. It seems that the show's look-alikes are being murdered.

Ellie's dying to see the ending of this serial killer's saga— she's just praying that she's not part of the final episode.

Available February 2000 at your favorite retail outlet.

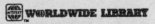

DEATH BY ACCIDENT

BILL CRIDER

A SHERIFF DAN RHODES MYSTERY

Accidents happen,
as the saying goes. But three
fatal accidents don't happen
within days of each other—
at least, not in Blacklin County, Texas.

First, John West was burned to a crisp
when he was hit by a car while holding
a can of gasoline. Then Pep Yeldell,
best known for stealing cars and
wives, drowned in an old swimming pool.

Sheriff Dan Rhodes has a hunch that these
two deaths were murder. A third body makes
three too many and puts Rhodes onto the
cleverly concealed trail of a killer.

Available March 2000 at your favorite retail outlet.

 W(O)RLDWIDE LIBRARY®

Visit us at www.worldwidemystery.com

WBC343

The Girl at the End of the Line

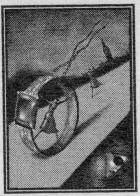

Charles Mathes

A MOLLY & NELL O'HARA MYSTERY

When Nell O'Hara and older sister Molly discover that their grandmother died under suspicious circumstances, they decide it's time to find out why sudden death seems to run in their family.

An old Broadway playbill leads them to secrets of their grandmother's scandalous past. The sisters follow a trail of adventure and mystery that sweeps from America to England, and finally to a secluded island on the Atlantic coast where a chilling legacy of murder awaits....

Available March 2000 at your favorite retail outlet.

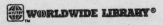

WORLDWIDE LIBRARY®